A NIGHT TO REMEMBER

"Now, turn out the light, will you?" Marc said laconically.

Dana did that without comment and stretched out carefully on her edge of the mattress, doing her best to avoid touching his body.

There were several moments of silence and then Marc let out an exasperated sigh before his arm snaked out and pulled her tightly against him. "The object of the arrangement was to get you warm," he said in the vicinity of her ear as he maneuvered her spoon-fashion against his long body. "And stop squirming, for God's sake."

"I'm not squirming—"

"Well, whatever you call it. If you want to keep everything on a nice platonic level—just breathe. Get it?"

Dana took a deep breath and finally muttered, "Got it. I wasn't trying anything."

"I know that," he growled. "The object of this exercise is to exchange body heat in a gentlemanly way. If you keep breaking the rules, I'll toss you back to your bed or . . ."

"Or what?" she asked daringly.

The Temporary Bride

by

Glenna Finley

A SIGNET BOOK

SIGNET
Published by the Penguin Group
Penguin Books USA Inc., 375 Hudson Street,
New York, New York 10014, U.S.A.
Penguin Books Ltd, 27 Wrights Lane,
London W8 5TZ, England
Penguin Books Australia Ltd, Ringwood,
Victoria, Australia
Penguin Books Canada Ltd, 10 Alcorn Avenue,
Toronto, Ontario, Canada M4V 3B2
Penguin Books (N.Z.) Ltd, 182–190 Wairau Road,
Auckland 10, New Zealand

Penguin Books Ltd, Registered Offices:
Harmondsworth, Middlesex, England

First published by Signet, an imprint of New American Library,
a division of Penguin Books USA Inc.

First Printing, August, 1993
10 9 8 7 6 5 4 3 2 1

PUBLISHER'S NOTE
This is a work of fiction. Names, characters, places, and incidents either
are the product of the author's imagination or are used fictitiously, and
any resemblance to actual persons, living or dead, events, or locales is
entirely coincidental.

BOOKS ARE AVAILABLE AT QUANTITY DISCOUNTS WHEN USED TO PROMOTE
PRODUCTS OR SERVICES. FOR INFORMATION PLEASE WRITE TO PREMIUM
MARKETING DIVISION, PENGUIN BOOKS USA INC., 375 HUDSON STREET, NEW
YORK, NEW YORK 10014.

If you purchased this book without a cover you should be aware that this
book is stolen property. It was reported as "unsold and destroyed" to the
publisher and neither the author nor the publisher has received any
payment for this "stripped book."

Brightly dawns our wedding day;
Joyous hour, we give thee greeting!
Whither, whither art thou fleeting?
Fickle moment, prithee stay!

—W. S. Gilbert, 1885

Chapter One

It was past even the fashionably late hour for dinner by the time Dana McIntyre paid off her taxi and walked wearily into her small hotel in Asheville, North Carolina.

Even at that time of night, the July heat and humidity remained stubbornly in place, leaving Dana with two things in mind: a long cool bath followed by a glass filled with ice cubes and whatever was in her room's minibar. Only then would she contemplate struggling down to the coffee shop for food.

The lobby was clean but hardly inspiring, with potted palms tucked between rattan sofas and a country-western song coming from a corner speaker as she approached the counter for her key. In the interval before the clerk got off the telephone, Dana heard at least one chorus about how "she got the gold mine but I got the shaft" with a soulful guitar accompaniment, and started to laugh despite her mood.

Her chuckle made the young clerk abruptly terminate his phone call and assume a business-like tone. "Could I help you?"

"I'd like my key, please. Room 301."

His hand hovered in front of the box with her key and he frowned as he turned back, keeping the key clutched in his hand. "Your name, please."

At any other time, Dana would have been annoyed by his officious manner, but at that moment, she didn't want the slightest hitch in getting to her room where she could take off her shoes and collapse. "McIntyre," she replied in a carefully level voice. "Dana McIntyre. I checked in yesterday."

Her restrained reply made him nod hastily and reach over to the switchboard. "There have been several calls for you, Miss McIntyre. I had no way of knowing when you'd return."

His manner had changed by then from uncertain authority to frank admiration as his glance swept over her, lingering on her collar-length chestnut-brown hair with reddish highlights. Her dark blue eyes were staring back at him with some impatience, he noted, and the lips which had earlier curved with laughter were starting to clamp in a straight line.

By then, the music had changed to a baritone announcing that "if the phone don't ring, you'll know it's me," and Dana unconsciously considered it remarkably apt in the circumstances.

The young clerk tried to sound businesslike as his glance dropped to the messages he was still clutching in his hand. "They're all from a Mr. Elliott."

The sound of Marc Elliott's name brought a

sudden twinge of dismay to Dana's midsection—
a part of her anatomy that was already protesting the lack of dinner. What in the dickens
was her brother's partner calling her about? Unless something had happened to Keith.

"He wants you to meet him tomorrow," the
clerk was going on as he frowned down at the
slips. "He said something about not being able
to get in touch with you any more today."

"Oh, Lord. Now what?" Dana was unaware
that she'd spoken aloud until she saw the clerk's
surprised expression. "Never mind," she said,
managing to smile as she reached out for the key
and the messages. "I'll do some phoning when I
get up in my room. Are they still serving in the
coffee shop?"

"Actually, they'll be closing in about ten minutes," he said importantly, consulting his watch.
"I suppose you could have room service though,
if you called down right away."

"I'll do that. Thanks," she said, turning
toward the elevators without wasting any more
time.

Once she arrived at her room, she only paused
long enough to kick off her shoes before phoning
down to order a club sandwich and a pot of coffee. Then, she shoved a pillow behind her on the
bed and pulled the phone in her lap to call her
brother's apartment in Dallas.

She didn't realize she'd been holding her
breath, hoping for an answer, until the receiver
was lifted and she heard his impatient "Hello."

"If you greet your girlfriends in that tone, your

datebook is going to be full of blank pages," Dana told him with sisterly candor.

"I'd be quaking in my boots if I had any on," Keith replied. "You caught me on the way to the shower. Are you still in Asheville?"

"I was the last time I looked out the window." She paused and then went to the heart of the matter. "Are you all right?"

"Other than freezing to death since I'm standing under the air-conditioning vent—I think so. Why? What's on your mind?"

"Well, I just got back to the hotel and found a sheaf of messages from your partner."

"Marc!" There was a perceptible pause. Then, "I'll be damned. I wondered why he wanted to know where you were when he called this morning. It's not as if you kept in touch with each other these days."

Dana could feel warmth creeping under her cheekbones after that announcement. Keith was exhibiting more tact than usual since he knew that not only did she not keep in touch with Marcus Elliott—she made damned sure that they seldom came within hailing distance.

"Look, if you're going into a brown study, do it on your own or at least let me get a robe," Keith complained.

"No—that's all I had to say. Actually, I thought something might have happened to you. But since there's nothing more wrong than usual, I'll let you go."

"Wait a minute—before you hang up. You

might get in touch with me when you find out what Marc has on his mind."

"Why don't you just call across town and ask him?"

"Because he's out of town, sister mine. Somewhere near your neighborhood. It's to do with some clients of ours in Kentucky. Anyhow, let me know if you change your itinerary. Okay?"

"Okay. Bye for now," she said absently as she put the receiver down and sat frowning at the clock on the bedside table. Then her gaze went down to the messages she had dropped beside the phone and her frown deepened. Why in the world would Marc be trying to get in touch with her if it weren't anything to do with Keith. It had been months since he'd made any attempt to deal with her personally.

She grimaced then and got to her feet, going over to the window and staring down through the dusk onto a very unscenic parking lot. Not that she could blame him for keeping a safe distance after what had happened on their first and only date, shortly after he and Keith had formed their legal partnership. She'd heard about his popularity with the female sex from Keith, who'd known him since college. Apparently his reputation hadn't diminished in that regard in the years that had passed. It wasn't surprising, Dana had to admit as she leaned wearily against the window. The man was tall, lean, fair-haired, and in his mid-thirties. He was also, she remembered, stubborn, cynical, and not the type to suf-

fer fools gladly. And for the word *fool*—just
substitute the name Dana McIntyre.

Admittedly she'd acted like an idiot on that
date as she chose to ignore the ten-year age difference between them. Trying for instant sophis-
tication to impress him, she'd worn a dress that
had made her brother frown reprovingly when
she'd emerged to meet Marc in the front hall.
She'd capped her performance by talking nonstop and drinking too much champagne after
dinner. As a result, Marc practically had to carry
her out of his car at midnight to deposit her back
at her brother's apartment where she'd been
spending the weekend. Even that wasn't the
worst of it, she remembered, stifling an urge to
groan as the memory came back. After their arrival, she'd lingered in the foyer and proclaimed
loudly to her brother that she'd never go out
with the man again. Then she'd turned around
to find Marc emerging from the study where
he'd gone to make a phone call.

There hadn't been a word said from that point
on. She'd managed to disappear into the bedroom, wishing she could sink into a deep hole
instead of an innerspring mattress.

The next morning, Keith hadn't hesitated to
tell her what an idiot she'd been. Since she'd
been suffering from the grandmother of all hangovers as well as a guilty conscience, she hadn't
contradicted him. Later, when she'd tried to pen
an apology, her determination had given out. Especially when she heard that Marc had phoned
Keith earlier that morning to report he was fly-

ing out to Los Angeles to advise one of their clients in some litigation.

Sensing a reprieve, Dana had quietly headed home, deciding that fate had taken pity on her. Since then, she'd made sure that her path hadn't crossed Marc's again—especially with her unspoken apology still in abeyance. Why he wanted to get in touch with her now left her shaking her head.

At that moment, a knock on the door announced the arrival of her room service tray and it was a relief to contemplate something pleasant—like a thick sandwich and some hot coffee.

Her anticipatory smile faded quickly when she opened the door and found a familiar six-foot figure waiting impatiently in the hallway. His attention wasn't on her though, but was centered on a toddler who was across the way happily pushing all the buttons on the soft drink machine.

"Cut that out, John!" Marc said in stentorian tones that should have had the sturdy, towheaded youngster freezing in his tracks. Instead, he looked over his shoulder, grinned engagingly, and went back to pushing the buttons.

"I warned you, young man," Marc said, starting toward him, obviously intent on enforcing his command.

The next thing Dana knew she had cut him off, saying frantically, "Don't you dare spank him. He's too little and besides, he probably doesn't understand."

"I wasn't going to spank him," Marc said irritably, removing her hand from his arm so he could reach down and separate the youngster from the vending machine's knobs. "No more fizzy stuff till after your dinner," he informed him. "Then we'll see. Okay?"

Reluctantly the toddler nodded. "Okay, nunc."

Dana's lips parted in amazement. "Nunc?"

"He can't say uncle," Marc said, swinging the boy into his arms. "Could we continue this conversation in your room," he asked when a couple coming down the hall lingered to give them a curious look. "Otherwise, we might as well sell tickets."

That remark made the couple move on quickly to the elevator while Dana found herself trailing him back to her room. Once inside, Marc carefully closed the door and went over to deposit young John on a chair in front of the television. A moment or two later, he'd found a cartoon show which immediately made the boy change to practically a graven image in the chair.

Dana was watching the tableau with disbelief, only sinking onto the edge of the nearest bed when her tired feet reminded her that she'd walked too far during the day. She waited until Marc gave an audible sigh of satisfaction before she said, "Now, would you tell me what the——" Marc's warning frown made her remember the young ears practically within spitting distance. She hastily changed her sentence structure. ". . . what in the world is going on?"

"I tried calling you. You were never in." Marc

obviously debated moving the only unoccupied chair from the window area and then settled for the end of her bed.

"That's the point of vacations. In Asheville," she told him wearily, "you don't hang around hotel rooms if you've come to visit Biltmore."

"So that's where you were all day—touring at the Vanderbilt mansion. I should have known."

"Umm." With some difficulty, she restrained herself from asking exactly why he should have known since he hadn't shown the slightest interest in her whereabouts over the past weeks. Deciding that such a comment might indicate that she'd wondered about his pointed lack of attention, she decided to take the offensive. Her glance went over to appraise the sturdy little boy completely engrossed in the cartoons and then turned back to Marc. "I didn't think you were the baby-sitting type."

"You didn't stick around long enough to find out much of anything. My sister and brother-in-law live about fifty miles from here most of the time."

It was the last part of his sentence that kept Dana from interrupting. Instead, she frowned thoughtfully and waited for him to continue.

His hand went up to knead the muscles at the back of his neck as he said, "My brother-in-law had to go up to New York to submit some plans—he's an architect—and lost out to a cab when he was trying to cross a street last night."

"Oh, Lord," Dana said with an indrawn breath, "he wasn't—"

"—killed?" Marc cut in. "No, thank God. A broken leg, but they're keeping him in the hospital to make sure there are no internal injuries. I was spending the weekend with Sue before driving to Lexington to see a client." He gave Dana a thoughtful look. "Did you know about that from Keith?"

She nodded. "I called him when I got back here tonight. He knew about your trip but not any of the rest of it."

"Probably because he doesn't have Sue's number. Anyhow, I drove Sue to the airport to be with her husband but that left you-know-who—" he jerked his head toward the small boy in the chair, "without a chaperone. At least for a day or two. Sue's mother will fly in from the West Coast to take over after that. In the meantime . . ."

As his voice trailed off suggestively, the gist of his conversation finally registered on Dana. She drew in her breath sharply and glanced over toward the still little figure in the chair. "Well, obviously you couldn't leave him alone, but surely you've been with him before. How old is he anyhow?"

There had been a commercial break in the cartoon program, long enough for John to turn to her with a wide smile and hold up a finger on each hand. "Two. John two," he proclaimed before turning back to the television.

"And one month," Marc said.

"Well, then—I don't see your problem."

Marc's eyebrows drew together. "My problem," he said, putting a sarcastic emphasis on the last word, "is that it's going to be difficult to carry him into the business appointments I have scheduled in Lexington tomorrow." As he saw her open her mouth to protest he went on doggedly, "I can't very well cancel them because one of the men is on his way over from Belgium at the moment. Fortunately, I remembered Keith saying that you were vacationing in this part of the country. You are on a holiday, aren't you?"

"Well, sort of. Maybe a busman's holiday. That's why I was checking out the interiors at Biltmore today. There's some art deco there that's simply superb."

Marc nodded, his frown smoothing as he changed position on the end of the bed, trying to get comfortable. "I remember now. You are an interior designer, aren't you?"

Since she had babbled on about her job for fully half the night on that miserable date she'd had with him, it wasn't surprising that he remembered. "That's right. The company's located in north Dallas."

His eyebrows went up. "I thought it was Houston. Keith didn't mention that you'd moved."

That was because she'd told Keith that if he talked about it, she'd make his life miserable, Dana recalled with satisfaction. Certainly she hadn't wanted Marc to think that she was now in the neighborhood and panting for another chance to go out with him.

"Do you go into these brown studies often, or just when you're around me?" Marc's tone was annoyed. "You seem in as much of a fog as John over there. At least he has the television as an excuse."

"Sorry," she said lightly. "I was up at the crack of dawn today so I could walk miles at Biltmore. All I planned for tonight was a nice warm bath and some dinner——" Her comments were interrupted by a knock on the door. "That must be dinner now," she said, getting to her feet. "I'm sorry to interrupt all this but—"

"Relax. I managed to combine our room service orders," Marc said, getting to the door first and opening it to admit the waiter poised beside a wheeled drop-leaf table. "Come in," he invited, waving a hand toward the window at the far side of the room. "Anywhere over there will be fine."

Dana watched open-mouthed as the table went past. John merely craned his neck when his view of the television was momentarily blocked and then paid no attention to the man arranging the plates.

"One club sandwich, coffee, one pizza and beer, and one peanut butter and jelly sandwich with a glass of milk," the waiter said, surveying it all with satisfaction. "'Is that right, sir?"

"It looks fine," Marc said, deftly signing the check and ushering him out. "Thanks very much. We'll leave it in the hall when we're finished."

At that juncture the cartoon program ended and the picture changed to a dull commercial. Young John squirmed off his chair and came over to inspect the laden table with interest.

"Lunch was a long time ago," Marc explained

as he turned his nephew gently. "John, this is Dana. Can you say hello?"

Dana felt herself being inspected in the calm, noncommittal fashion that children take as a matter of course and wisely didn't make any advances. For some reason, she also found herself holding her breath before the toddler announced solemnly, "Dan-Dan," and then "Me eat now."

"Dan-Dan!" Dana repeated, and then shrugged as both John and Marc turned to survey dinner. Her gaze sharpened as John struggled up to kneel on a chair and appropriated part of her club sandwich. "Hey, wait a minute— you're supposed to be eating peanut butter."

The toddler's vocabulary might have been limited, but there was no doubt that he understood because his grip tightened on her sandwich and a look of stubborn determination came over his face.

"Now look what you've done," Marc complained blandly as he selected a sizeable portion of steaming pizza and inspected it with satisfaction. "The little guy obviously prefers a club sandwich—"

"Except for lettuce and the tomato," Dana said, watching the dissection that was going on between chubby fingers.

"That's all right. He'll survive on turkey and bacon," Marc commented, taking another bite of pizza. "Do you like pizza?"

"Of course, but—"

Dana's puzzled reply was cut off when Marc went on as if she hadn't spoken, "In that case, you'd better share this with me. Believe me, there's no point in ruffling you-know-who's feathers now. He's short an afternoon nap and that's murder."

Having delivered that commentary, he reached for another portion of pizza. Dana made up her mind quickly and was right behind him. The way things were going, the menu choices were narrowing quickly and she wasn't keen on what would be available to latecomers. The first bite of pizza was a pleasant surprise. "Ummm. This is good!"

Marc nodded, putting his piece down on a plate while he opened the bottle of beer and poured it into a glass. "We can divide this, too, if you like."

An unhappy murmur from the toddler at her elbow brought her attention down in time to see a glob of mayonnaise leave the club sandwich and drip through his tiny fingers onto his white shirt.

"Oh, help!" Dana hastily put her pizza slice onto a saucer and made a grab for the disintegrating sandwich, ignoring John's loud protest as he saw his dinner being snatched away.

"Look, sweetie—I'm sorry. I'll give it back," Dana assured him hastily as she put the sandwich alongside her piece of pizza. "You have to be cleaned up." A quick swipe with a paper napkin showed that it was not a permanent solution. "Just a minute. I'll get a damp towel, love. Stay there and don't move."

"I'll get it," Marc told her, following on her heels. "At least, let me help."

"It would be more help if you'd brought a bib in the first place," Dana said over her shoulder as she reached the bathroom basin and moistened the end of a towel.

"We packed in a hurry. Obviously, Sue's mind wasn't on details."

His quiet reply brought a twinge of remorse to Dana as she emerged clutching the towel. "I'm sorry. It's just that I'm not used to dealing with the younger set." Her gaze took in the scene at the table as she spoke and then she made a dash for the small figure reaching for the tall glass. "No, no, John. You can't have the beer." She pulled him back on the chair. "The milk belongs to you, but not until I get rid of the mayonnaise on your fingers. What are you doing?" The last came as she felt Marc kneeling at her side.

"Relax. I'm just trying to salvage a slice of tomato. It isn't doing a thing for the rug. What did you throw it down for, John?"

"Me no like," was that stalwart's reply from the chair.

"Well, me no like it on the rug."

"You're not supposed to talk baby talk," Dana said, cutting into Marc's stern reply. "Otherwise, how do they learn?"

"I thought you said you didn't know anything about kids."

"Everybody reads magazines," she told him before turning back to the fair-haired little boy.

"Now look, sweetie. Hold still while I try to clean your hands and then your shirt."

She found herself staring into a pair of blue eyes with a direct gaze that was disconcertingly like his uncle's before he lowered it to solemnly observe her ministrations. The hands cleaned up fine, but the shirt was another story. "That looks awful," she concluded, staring at the grease spot decorating the front of the little white shirt. "He can't go around looking like that."

Marc bent over and put the glass of milk to John's lips. "Well, fortunately his social schedule is nil for the rest of the night. Maybe you can do some running repairs by morning."

"Me!" Dana's response came out a full octave higher than her usual tones. "What are you talking about?'

Marc shook his head and gave her a warning glance before turning back to John, who was pushing away the glass of milk. "How about some peanut butter sandwich?" he asked his nephew.

"Me stop now," came the decided reply.

"He can't do that," Dana protested. "A quarter of a club sandwich isn't a decent meal for a youngster."

Since John had decided that he'd have some potato chips for dessert, Marc sighed and then picked up a section of the untouched peanut butter sandwich and waved it in front of the youngster. "C'mon—give this a chance. It's good!"

John scrunched back as far in the chair as he could manage, as he uttered a definite "No."

Then, as if adults required a longer reply, he went on patiently, "Me no want."

Marc straightened, still clutching the sandwich. "Okay," he said, looking at Dana. "Now what do you suggest?"

She raised her hands in surrender. "How about the two of us splitting that sandwich. I'm still hungry."

"What about the nutrition bit you were going on about? Although I'm not surprised that you're changing your tactics. I told Keith . . ." His voice trailed off as he realized that he was already waist-high in quicksand.

"I don't know what you're talking about," Dana cut in angrily. It didn't take an Einstein to realize that his discussion with her brother had probably made her sound like the wicked witch of the north. She wasn't surprised, but that didn't make it hurt any the less. She lifted her chin. "I'm not brain-dead, Mr. Elliott, no matter what you think. I know I didn't help my cause that night—" There was a pause as she tried for more gracious phrasing and then decided it was as close to an apology as he was going to get. "—that night we went out." A look of intense concentration on John's face gave her a legitimate chance to change the subject. "Are you wet?" she asked him.

There was pronounced pause while the toddler reviewed his options. Then he shook his head and gestured toward the television saying, "More toons."

"He's lying in what few teeth he has," Marc

said. "Fortunately, my sister shoved a box of diapers in the van at the last minute."

"Then I think you'd better get them out of the van. The sooner the better," Dana said, watching the little boy squirm on his chair.

"It won't take long. Just keep an eye on him for a minute or so."

"It'll take you longer than that to get down to the parking lot," Dana said in a brisk tone. "Are you sure that he won't feel he's been abandoned with a stranger?"

"The only trouble you'll have with him now is if you suddenly turn off the tube," Marc assured her, as he jerked a thumb at his nephew who was giggling at the antics of a giant mouse. "Besides, I've got the diapers right next door. Actually, it would be a lot more convenient if I just go through here."

Without waiting for her comment, he walked over to a door in the middle of the wall by the television console and pulled it wide to show that he'd already unbolted the door on the other side.

"Hold on a minute." After her initial surprise, Dana was on his heels following him. "You mean that this is your room?"

Marc bestowed a disgusted look over his shoulder as he unzipped some luggage on a table near the window. "Well, if I planned a career of breaking and entering, I sure wouldn't start with a hotel like this."

"What's wrong with it?" The words were out before she knew it and she waved a hand to try and push them away. "I mean—I don't care about the hotel. Why are you even in it, especially in the room next to mine?"

"Because I need your help. At least for the next day or so. Keith is always telling me that you're a patsy to anybody with a problem—now's your chance to prove it."

"I presume that you mean you need a baby-sitter. That hardly comes in the problem category. Besides, I told you—I don't know anything about small children. Keith and I haven't any near relatives with the patter of tiny feet around—" She broke off her objections as it suddenly occurred to her that there was now a heavy silence in the room behind her. Apparently John had discovered the off switch on the television. Hurrying back into her room, she discovered him standing at the end of the bed with a woebegone look on his little face.

"Dan-Dan play me?" he asked hopefully.

The mournful blue eyes combined with the stained shirt and socks falling to half-mast over his ankles were an unbeatable combination.

Dana found herself on her knees in front of him, saying, "Sweetie, maybe we can play later. Right now, you need a bath. Let's look and see if there's something that floats so you can play in there. Would you like that?"

"Sounds good to me." It was Marc responding from where he stood in the doorway between the two rooms. "I'll find his sleepwear and fix up his bed. Okay?"

If he'd exhibited the slightest satisfaction in

his voice, Dana would have been tempted to say she'd changed her mind. But his glance was simply frank and grateful.

A tug on her hand showed that the younger family member was impatient. "Me play."

"Not yet, young man. I'll start filling the tub and get you respectable before the fun starts."

This seemed to be all right with John, especially when she let him help pour in a package of bubble bath that she found among the other complimentary toiletries displayed on the vanity. After watching the bubbles materialize, John could hardly wait to get in with them, and he accepted the slight delay while he was being deprived of his clothes and wet diaper on the bath mat with cheerful aplomb.

Marc didn't reappear with a clean diaper until his nephew had been lowered into the water and was happily using the face cloth to smother the bubbles within reach.

"Haven't you found any bath toys?" Dana asked Marc, as she got up from her knees alongside the tub, finding it wasn't easy after a day of walking around Biltmore. "Capturing bubbles with you-know-what isn't going to last long."

"There's nothing in his bag that floats—I looked. How about your stuff?"

"I can't think of anything." Dana took a quick glance down and encountered John's rapidly darkening one. "It's all right, honey. I'll bet I can find something. You stay here," she told Marc. "You might even use that face cloth to wash the pizza off his chin."

Marc looked at his nephew and shook his head. "I'll wait until he's finished with the bubbles. There's no point in upsetting the status quo."

Dana gave a resigned nod. "You're probably right. I'll see what I can find."

She was back in a couple of minutes triumphantly waving a plastic cup. "Pay dirt."

"I'm not sure pine bubble bath will do much for your next coffee break," Marc said with a considering look.

"So I start an expense account," she told him and handed it over as John said decisively, "Nunc play me."

"I think that's a splendid idea," she announced. "We'll need some extra towels. I'll go in your room," she continued with a bland look at Marc, "and pick up some extras."

"How about calling housekeeping and asking them to bring some more?" Marc's request caught her before she could cross the threshold and escape. "That way, everybody will be happy. Hey—cut it out!"

The last came as John decided it was more fun to dump water from his new cup outside the tub and, in the process, managed to fill his uncle's shoe.

"I'll ask for an extra bath mat, as well," Dana said, doing her best to keep a straight face. "Don't forget to wash his chin."

Her shoulders were still shaking with laughter as she returned a minute or two later and dropped two more towels around the bathroom door. "I'll call housekeeping," she promised from a safe distance, and made a hasty exit as she heard Marc protest when more water came over the edge.

She was reading the newspaper, comfortably propped against the headboard of her bed, five minutes later when a small naked body dashed out of the bathroom and made straight for her. A disheveled Marc was close on John's heels, clutching a towel. "Hold on there, chum," he ordered as the toddler went headfirst into the side of the mattress, flinging his arms over Dana's knees. "You'll catch cold. I haven't finished drying you yet."

Dana looked ruefully down at her skirt as she put the paper aside. "He's a lot drier now." Then, reaching down for the slippery little boy, she pulled him up on the bed and put out a hand for Marc's towel. "I can take care of the finishing touches. That's if I can find him." Tossing the towel over the toddler's head, she said. "Where did John go? I can't see him."

"Me here," the boy crowed, pulling the towel off promptly.

"So I see," Dana said, smiling. "C'mon—let's get you dry before you catch pneumonia. Hey—hold still. Maybe you can manage a pair of pajamas or something," she said, bestowing a fleeting glance at Marc, who lingered by the end of the bed. Then, giving a longer look at his drenched shirt front and trousers, she added solemnly, "Perhaps one for each of you."

"That had occurred to me," he replied, matching her tone. "I'll be back with John's just as soon as I dig them out."

A small pair of blue cotton knit pajamas were tossed on the end of the bed a minute or two later as Marc poked his head around the door frame. "Give me a minute or two to dry off and I'll come and swab out your bathroom."

He had disappeared before Dana could say it wasn't necessary. After she'd persuaded John to don the pajamas, she peered inside the bathroom to find a brush for his hair and drew a breath of surprise at the chaos. Puddles of water were all over the tile floor, allowing the soggy bath mat to float into the corner. She shook her head and backed out hastily, deciding to use the comb in her purse for John's rumpled hair.

She'd just finished and was beaming at the adorable picture he presented when Marc reappeared stripped to the waist and wearing only a pair of worn jeans. "I didn't see any point in getting anything else wet," he told Dana, lifting his nephew from his Buddha-like perch on the bedspread. "Next time I'm close to you in a bathtub, young man, I'll wear a wet suit."

"Which is what you ended up with this time," Dana said, not bothering to hide her smile.

"Right. Say good night to . . ." he paused and then added, grinning, "Dan-Dan."

His nephew squirmed rebelliously in his arms. "No. Dan-Dan play me."

"Nope. It's my turn now," Marc told him firmly, heading back to his room. "Dan-Dan play me." He turned to see Dana's puzzled expression. "In a manner of speaking. I need your help, so stick around."

Chapter Two

There was an outraged uproar from the other room when John was apparently deposited in the portable crib and told that he had to go to sleep. Dana could hear Marc making soothing noises and then came the sounds of surrender which involved picture books and stuffed toys in the crib, as well.

Dana grinned, delighted to find that Marc Elliott had joined the human race; as a carefree bachelor he'd been more familiar with discos than diapers. The realization that he'd had to change his reading material from *Playboy* to *Winnie the Pooh* was even more satisfying, and she relaxed against the headboard of her bed enjoying every moment.

When Marc reappeared he'd put on a sport shirt with his jeans. He carefully closed the connecting door between the rooms until it was just barely ajar.

"I still hear noises in there," Dana said, sitting up and stuffing the pillow more comfortably behind her.

"That's because John's carrying on a conversation with a panda, a dog, and a train engine," Marc said, going over to the hall door and turning off the overhead light.

"Hey, what's going on?"

"Simmer down," he said in a tone that didn't brook any interference. "The darker it is in here, the sooner he'll go to sleep. I hope," he added, in a tone that had more than a touch of desperation in it. "Maybe you've gathered that I could use some help."

"You've just had a long day," Dana assured him, not wanting to appear too eager to be convinced. "He's as cute as a bug."

"A very energetic bug. Have you anything to make another cup of coffee?" he asked, subsiding on the foot of the bed. "I'm so tired I almost fell asleep while Tigger was still practicing short jumps."

Since he didn't look as if it would take him more than three or four minutes to revive, Dana heard that announcement with some skepticism. "I should have thought that baby-sitting for your nephew would be a piece of cake for you."

"I wish to hell you wouldn't mention food," he complained. "The last bit of that peanut butter and jelly sandwich didn't do much to fill the cracks. You wouldn't have anything packed away, would you?"

"There are some chocolate chip cookies in my tote bag," Dana admitted, aware that she had a few gaping cracks, as well.

"Great! Didn't I see an immersion heater and some instant coffee on the shelf in the closet?"

"For just walking through the place, you didn't miss much," she told him, getting to her feet and heading for the provisions. "I only have one plastic cup, though."

"How about a bathroom glass?" he countered. "I just happened—"

"I know. You just happened to see an extra one when you were in there with John."

He nodded complacently. "I'd offer the one in my room, but I don't want to tromp through while he's still awake."

Dana couldn't dispute the sense of that so she merely nodded and set about preparing their dessert course. Once Marc had his steaming glass of coffee on the table by the television and a modest pile of cookies beside it, he didn't waste any more time.

"I don't know how serious you are about this vacation of yours," he said, sounding once more like a busy corporate executive rather than an exhausted uncle. "I forgot to ask Keith, and anyhow, things have changed since I talked to him. Having John throws everything into a cocked hat unless you cooperate."

"Exactly what do you mean by 'cooperating'?" Dana asked with a frown.

Her suspicious tone evidently annoyed Marc because he scowled across at her and said, "Not what you're evidently thinking. I haven't gone in for any white slavery deals for at least two weeks. And you might give me credit for some subtlety—if I planned a Bacchanalian orgy, do you think I'd drag my nephew along as a cover? If that weren't enough, your brother happens to be my partner and my best friend, so even if you were Cleopatra stepping off the barge, I'd restrain myself. Now, what in the hell are you laughing about?"

Dana had trouble talking between chuckles. "You!" she told him succinctly. "I thought you were going to bring in the Bill of Rights as a clincher." When he opened his mouth to object, she put up her palms in protest. "Okay. You've convinced me that your motives are as pure as the driven snow. Anyhow, there's no need to gift-wrap your problem. I gather that you need a baby-sitter for John for a day or two. Now that I've met him, I'll be happy to go along with the idea, although if you need an experienced 'nanny' . . ." As he shook his head firmly, she broke off her sentence. "Where did I go wrong?" she asked a moment later.

"No nanny," he said. "I've been thinking, and it seems to me the best way to appear in Lexington is as a happy family group. Before John, you could have been a fiancée. With him, you'd better be my wife."

"Your *what*?"

Her surprised shriek was loud enough to bring new conversation from the next room, which translated to "Dan-Dan, come here!"

"Now see what you've done," Marc said irritably, getting to his feet. Then he sat down again as another "Dan-Dan" summons came in a louder tone. "It looks as if you're on," he told her. "And it serves you right. Tell him to go to sleep after you've convinced him that you're still alive."

Since he clearly had justice on his side, Dana slid off the bed and made her appearance in the other room.

John was standing in his crib, shaking the sides as he kept up a steady "Dan-Dan, Dan-Dan, Dan-Dan" in piercing tones. When he saw Dana approaching, he broke off to give her a big grin. "You play me?" he asked hopefully.

"Sweetie—no. It's too late. If you're not quiet, you're going to wake up those friends of yours. Now, if you'll lie down, I'll cover you all up again. And tomorrow," she said, getting in ahead before he could protest, "I promise, we'll play. Okay?"

The toddler appeared to consider his options and finally nodded. After assuring her that he needed to sleep with the metal train engine as well as all the stuffed toys, he settled down in the portable crib. When Dana blew him a kiss, he grinned again and managed a loud, smacking one in return.

His sweet expression brought unexpected tears to her eyes and she paused by the connecting door to dash them away before Marc saw how vulnerable she'd become.

In her absence, he'd moved from his chair to stretch out on the edge of the bed and it was with reluctance that he pushed himself upright to lean against the headboard.

"If this is your first step toward family togetherness, you can tear up your instruction book," Dana told him, firmly banishing any holdover sentiment.

"Don't be an idiot." Marc's tone matched hers for coldness. "If I planned on a weekend rendezvous, it wouldn't be with a two-year-old chaperone and a woman who'd announced she'd be happy if she never saw me again."

Dana felt a guilty flush on her cheekbones. "I meant to send you a note apologizing for that."

"It would have been nice. I didn't lose any sleep watching the mailbox, though." He gave her a look which was more pitying than anything else, merely shifting on the pillow behind his back to get more comfortable. "This 'family togetherness,' as you call it, shouldn't have to last more than a day or two in Kentucky. Normally you could just appear as a glamorous girlfriend, but John put paid to that so you can portray wedded bliss when I have to wine and dine our client." He rubbed the side of his nose reflectively. "Actually, it's probably turning out better than I planned. No one in his right mind would bring his wife and a two-year-old if he were doing a serious investigation of a client."

As he paused to reach for the cooled coffee at his elbow, Dana was able to interrupt. "You mean, that's what this is all about? Some client investigation?"

"You needn't sound so disdainful. This particular account pays a great deal of your brother's salary as well as mine. Not only that, there's something extremely fishy about their last quarter's balance sheets. If it keeps up, part of a multimillion dollar company will be headed for a chapter eleven. The rest of the stockholders don't propose to stand around and watch it happen without some kind of an investigation."

"And that's where I come in?"

A slight smile softened his austere features. "Hell, no! Not if you're planning on gumshoe stuff. Most of the time, you'll just be up front taking care of John."

Her lips came together in a disapproving line. "And the rest of the time?"

"You'll be taking care of me when we're being wined and dined by the chairman of the board."

"That's all?"

"Don't sound so disappointed. You'll be well paid," he drawled.

"That isn't what I meant," she protested.

"What exactly did you mean?"

Dana realized suddenly that she wasn't sure. Only that being a temporary baby-sitter to a two-year-old, even one as cuddly as John, wasn't what she'd hoped he had in mind.

"You're doing it again."

Marc's exasperated comment brought her back to the present.

"I don't know what you're talking about."

"I'm talking about your tendency to go into the stratosphere whenever I want some answers. Didn't you get enough sleep last night, or did touring Biltmore do you in today?"

"I had plenty of sleep," she told him tersely.

"If you must know, I thought I heard a sound from John."

"You did. He's been singing his version of B-I-N-G-O for the last five minutes." Marc's tone showed what he thought of that excuse. "Well, will you do it?"

"You mean, go with you to Kentucky?"

He let out a sigh that showed he was holding onto his temper with an effort. "That's the general idea."

"I guess so. Although it seems to me that you're going about it the hard way."

"After the last two or three minutes, I'm inclined to agree with you." He swung his feet to the floor and stood up. "You might as well go on the payroll right away. I have some calls to make and it would be easier to use the lobby phones," he said, making his way to her hall door. "I may be awhile. John will probably con you for some drinks of water, but don't let him get out of his crib."

"What if he needs changing?" she asked in a sudden panic before he could disappear into the hallway. Then, seeing his expression as he glanced over his shoulder, she said hurriedly, "Oh, go away. I'll figure it out."

"That's the girl," he said, keeping his voice low. "If you need more help, I'll buy you a book on child care that you can read tomorrow on the way to Kentucky."

It was lucky for him that he ducked out the door promptly before the shoe that Dana had left beside the bed hit the wood behind him.

He still hadn't returned two drinks of water and one diaper change later. By then, John had demanded that she also re-read his tattered copy of *The Little Engine That Could*. Since it had been a long day by that time, Dana mentally had Marc tied to the railroad tracks on the last time through the book. John must have realized her patience was wearing thin because when the little engine reached the bottom of the mountain he gave her a cherubic smile and subsided in his portable crib, not even stirring when she tucked his blanket carefully around him.

After that, it seemed silly to watch a late movie in her room. Especially since the only thing showing was an oriental monster extravaganza. If Marc came back to find her watching it, he would have no doubts about her intelligence.

She carefully donned a pair of pale yellow pajamas that were trimmed in eggshell satin and just happened to be the most attractive ones she owned. Not that she had any ulterior motive, she assured herself as she carefully arranged the thigh-length robe which matched them on the foot of the bed. It just made sense to be prepared in case John called out in the night and Marc was a heavy sleeper.

Closing her eyes on that rationalization, she wondered how she'd become such a proficient liar in such a short time.

It only took a half hour after awakening the next morning for Dana to realize that her usual schedule was shot to blazes. She had pretended she didn't hear the piping young tones from the adjoining room without any guilt whatsoever. After all, John had a perfectly good uncle sleeping nearby. When the toddler's tones increased in volume as she closed the bathroom door for her shower, she amended her thinking. Marc could only be trying to sleep with that uproar in his ears. She hummed happily in the shower as she thought about it.

Unfortunately, her euphoric state of mind didn't last long. As she emerged from the bathroom wrapped in a towel sarong-fashion, she encountered both her next-door neighbors sitting on the end of her bed staring at her.

"I thought you were going to help," Marc accused before she could inquire about their early drop-in visit.

"Well, I wasn't going to knock on the door of your bedroom to volunteer my services," she told him austerely while going over to drop a kiss on John's head as he wriggled down off the mattress onto the floor.

Marc watched him head for her bathroom before announcing, "He wants a bath."

"The last time I looked, we had two bathrooms," she informed him, setting off after the toddler to make sure he didn't come to any harm.

"Exactly." Marc stood up and tightened the belt on his travel robe, since it was obvious that the bottoms of his navy-blue pajamas were his only other clothing. "Right now, I plan to use mine to shower and shave."

"But I have to dress," Dana protested, trying

to keep a firm grip on her towel as she watched John inspect her wet shower curtain.

"I wouldn't recommend it until after his bath," Marc said heading for his room. "Otherwise, you'll have to do a complete change."

"What do you propose? That I just wear a towel while I'm supervising?"

He looked amused as he stopped by the connecting door long enough to glance at her over his shoulder. "If that's what you plan, I'd suggest a bigger towel. That one obviously isn't going to last the course. I'm sorry I don't have time to stick around and watch."

"Oh, funny. Very funny," she fumed, watching him close the door behind him. She remained where she was for a moment trying to figure out her best course of action until a demanding "Dan-Dan" brought her quickly to the bathroom where John was trying to shed his pajamas.

For the next fifteen minutes, Dana found that Marc was right again. The towel wasn't big enough, which caused an emergency change to her thigh-length travel robe while John waited impatiently. By then, there was enough water in the tub for him to be lifted in and start playing with a plastic soap container that Dana had found in her suitcase. As Marc had warned, his nephew soon found it was a lot more fun to scoop water onto Dana than keep it in the porcelain tub. Since he did it with the best will in the world, she couldn't protest too loudly and spoil his fun.

They were still giggling when Dana pulled him out of the bath and started to towel him dry. "Okay, I can take over now," came a familiar masculine voice behind her. "You go ahead and get dressed." Then, as Dana got to her feet, startled by Marc's reappearance, he let out a silent whistle as he surveyed the way her dampened nylon robe was clinging to her. "I'll take John into our room," he said hastily, as he noted her embarrassment. "Might as well. All his clothes are there anyhow. Give a whistle when you're ready to go down to breakfast," he added, catching John plus his damp towel up in his arms and beating a hasty retreat.

It took just a quick look in the bathroom mirror after she wiped the steam from it for Dana to let out a graphic but unladylike phrase as she surveyed her reflection. The way the dampened nylon robe was clinging to her body left absolutely nothing to the imagination. And as quick as Marc's glance had been, she knew beyond a doubt that his survey hadn't missed an inch of the goods on display.

"Damn! Damn! Damn!" she muttered in an undertone before shedding the robe and reaching for a dry towel. So much for any hope of dignity when she'd started the day in a costume that North Carolina authorities wouldn't have allowed in a strip club. Not that it was all her fault, she told herself as she slipped into clean underthings and finally trim-fitting white slacks and a royal blue and white sleeveless shirt. If the man had a decent bone in his body, he would have knocked before he came back into the room. And who would have thought that he could shower, shave, and change into khaki cotton pants and a short-sleeved sport shirt as fast as he did. The lingering scent of his citrus after-shave showed that he hadn't missed any of his usual routine, either. That made her glance at her watch and draw in her breath in surprise. Marc hadn't been such a quick change artist after all. She must have played with John longer than she'd thought.

Confirmation came a minute later with an impatient knock on the connecting door. "Are you about ready?" Marc asked, keeping carefully on the other side of the door. "John's starving and so am I."

"I think so," Dana called, going over to open the connecting door. She stepped back hurriedly when John galloped through it as fast as his chubby legs could carry him. He made a fast circuit of the room and then threw himself happily at Dana's knees.

"Dan-Dan play me," he said hopefully.

"No way," said Marc, stepping in before she could answer. "The only thing you're going to do now, young man, is to play soldiers with some toast and a boiled egg." He gave Dana an approving glance before he plucked his nephew away from her and started toward the hall door. "Will it take you long to pack?" he asked over his shoulder.

"About five minutes," she said, retrieving her purse from the bed table and following him.

"Do you have a key?" he wanted to know before he closed it behind them. Then, before she could answer he shrugged and added. "It doesn't matter. We left the connecting door open."

"All the comforts of home," Dana said drily, as she hurried after John down the hall. "Take it easy, love. Don't you want to push the elevator button?"

Naturally such an invitation stopped John from pushing the buttons on the soft drink machine and steered him in the approved direction.

"Smart. Very smart," Marc said in an amused undertone as he brought up the rear of the procession. "You're sure you've never done this before?"

"Quite sure. I did train as an account executive in advertising right after I got out of college. I don't think there's too much difference, do you? Diversion was the name of the game there, too."

Marc's eyebrows rose. "Obviously this isn't the kind of a discussion to have before even one cup of coffee. Why don't we talk about the weather. After John," he said, lifting him up so he could poke a chubby finger at the button, "calls the elevator."

It was absurd to try to enjoy a meal when there were so many interruptions that Dana was scarcely able to take two bites in succession. At least, she told herself, it made for a splendid diet. John's span of attention wandered constantly and happily, making it necessary to shovel bites of egg under various guises. She managed to camouflage them as tugboats and helicopters before retiring to let Marc show him the advantage of dunking toast fingers in egg yolk.

"Is that a natural talent of yours?" Dana asked Marc, smiling when there was a brief respite.

"Must be." He gestured toward her plate. "Don't waste any time. John's egg is almost gone."

"More coffee?" An elderly waitress beamed as she paused by their booth. Without waiting for an answer, she went on, "Such a sweet little boy of yours. And so well behaved! Not like some we have in here, I can tell you. It's nice to see parents accepting responsibility."

"Thanks." Marc said smoothly before Dana could open her mouth. "We try, don't we, darling?"

Dana was amazed at how easy it was to smile in response. "All the time. I don't think we'd better linger over coffee, though."

"Right." Marc nodded his agreement. "If you could just bring the check . . ." he suggested to the waitress.

"Of course. And I'll bet your little boy would like a balloon, too."

John insisted on taking his time over which color the balloon should be. After that, there was another five minutes used to convince him it should be tied around his wrist to make sure it got into the elevator with him.

"Either I didn't get enough sleep last night or I haven't been giving my sister enough credit for the past two years," Marc confessed to Dana as they went back up to their rooms. "Suddenly I'm ready to go back to bed."

"I know what you mean. All those points that my married friends have been harping on for years are beginning to make sense," Dana confirmed with a smile while keeping a weather eye on John and his balloon. "Are we going to flip for who gets to drive to Lexington?"

" 'Fraid not." Even though he tried, Marc wasn't able to get the proper amount of regret in his voice to be convincing. "I'm driving a rental van and I'm the only one signed onto it. Besides, you're doing a great job with John." He grinned down at her disarmingly. "I promise to take over at coffee break and lunch."

"I'll hold you to it." Dana was amazed that she was actually looking forward to the prospect of watching over the blond toddler at her side. "Unless you have some goodies in his luggage, we'd better detour for a few travel toys."

"You can look over the selection while I'm taking our bags down to the car and let me know what you think," Marc said as they stopped in front of his room and unlocked the door. "How long do you need?"

"Give me five minutes," Dana asked, lingering by their connecting door. "I'll take over with our balloon boy then."

"Right." Marc put out a restraining hand when his nephew started to follow her. "John, can you help me put your toys in the bag?"

Dana took the opportunity to escape into her

room and do a final look around after stuffing the last things in her bag. A few minutes later, they persuaded John to change his venue and let Marc start packing the van with the luggage.

On the final trip out, when Dana pulled up at the cashier's desk, Marc shook his head. "I've taken care of all that."

"I didn't want you to pay my bills," she retorted, ignoring his hand which was urging her forward.

"Don't be silly." His tone was the familiar autocratic one that Dana remembered all too well. "You're doing me a favor. Just think of it as a business expense that I'm responsible for."

He could have talked all morning and not reminded her so forcefully that theirs was strictly a temporary business agreement, she thought. Which should convince her to keep all her new feelings to herself. It was hard, since John was an absolute darling and Marc was just the kind of man that any woman would have killed to have as an escort. When everybody insisted on regarding them as a "happy family," it was doubly hard, Dana acknowledged.

After loading the van, he should have looked as rumpled as she already felt. It was going to be another scorcher of a day and she envied John his pair of red shorts, T-shirt, and sandals. She crossed her fingers hoping that the air conditioner in the car would keep her from resembling a boiled lobster before noon.

"You're certainly quiet all of a sudden," Marc remarked after putting John in his seat in the middle and then motioning her in beside him. "Keith didn't tell me that you were one of those women who sulked."

"My brother would be more apt to tell you that I'm the type to go for the jugular," Dana said sweetly. "At least when we were growing up. Before you get behind the wheel, I need John's toys."

On hearing her request, the toddler beamed. "Dan-Dan play game."

"We'll see," she said, falling back on the old standby. "It depends on what's in the bag."

That comment came when Marc ceremoniously deposited a small canvas bag in her lap before going around to get in the driver's seat. "Everybody set?" he wanted to know, turning the ignition key. "Next stop, morning coffee in about an hour and a half."

Dana was ready for a stimulant of some kind when he pulled into a fast-food restaurant right on schedule. John had played with toy trucks for a few minutes and then gravitated to a book of stickers. By the time they stopped, everything and everybody within his arm's reach was decorated with dinosaurs and cartoon characters.

It was on the way through the restaurant door that Dana discovered one green brontosaurus still decorating the back of Marc's sleeve and pulled him to a stop so that she could peel it off. "I don't think you need this as part of your wardrobe," she told him, tossing it in the nearest litter barrel.

"Thanks." He grinned and then transferred

John's sturdy body from his arms to hers. "Take over, will you? I need to make a phone call. How about ordering a muffin and coffee for me. I'll settle our finances when I get back." Seeing John's rapt attention on the playground outside, "It looks as if that might be the easiest place to eat."

As John squirmed impatiently in her arms, Dana nodded. "We'll be there," she said, and headed for the counter before John started protesting.

He was happily ensconced in a netted play area and throwing plastic balls in every direction when Marc reappeared and sat down beside Dana at a table close by the children's section. "We're all set for dinner tonight," he told Dana, picking up his coffee cup with an approving nod. "I've arranged to hand John over to his grandmother tomorrow morning, too. She said that my brother-in-law is out of danger so there's no need for her to stay on at the hospital with my sister."

"Are you sure?" Dana asked, sounding doubtful.

"She was very definite about it. John will like it, too. They're great pals. Anyhow, she'll be in Lexington at our motel right on schedule." He gave Dana a quizzical look. "You don't appear delighted. I thought you'd have a different reaction."

"That just shows that you can't tell anything about the feminine sex." Dana kept her tone deliberately light to hide her disappointment at his newest announcement. "I don't know why you're surprised. John is a real two-year-old charmer."

"That little girl he's pelting with those balls

wouldn't agree with you," Marc said, nodding toward the play area. "It's a good thing his aim is so bad."

"She doesn't seem to object to his attention," Dana observed. "He'll be a real threat when he's twenty-one." She was tempted to add that it ran in the family but had enough sense to stifle the impulse. Marc Elliott's ego certainly didn't need any stoking where women were concerned.

If he wondered why she'd abruptly terminated the conversation, he didn't let on. Instead, he simply took a last swallow of coffee before saying, "We'd better hit the road again. I don't want to be late for our dinner date with George."

"George?"

"George Gonzalez—*Jorge*, to be accurate. Although in this country he prefers the anglicized version. He's the man who's CEO for the company I'm checking out."

"And the one you plan to impress with the wife and kiddie bit."

Marc's eyebrows went up in reproof. "If you want to put it that way."

"I've always believed in telling the truth."

"Always?" His expression was as skeptical as his tone.

Dana couldn't see any point in dragging out that conversation. Instead, she opted for a diplomatic change of subject. "I'd better rescue John. He's down so deep in that sea of balls that only his nose is showing."

"I'll do it." Marc sounded fed up all of a sudden. "Finish your coffee and then let's get going."

The armed verbal standoff continued until they arrived in Lexington that afternoon. Fortunately, John was too young to notice the labored attempts at social conversation which seldom got beyond the state of the weather or the changing scenery on either side of the road.

There was a half-hearted truce when Marc had to ask Dana to navigate in order to find the motel where he'd made a reservation for them to spend the night.

John was adamant about getting out of the car when it came time for Marc to go in and register. The lobby of the building was almost deserted, with only two attractive young women behind the registration desk. Dana was busy keeping John from cracking his head on the marble floor as he attempted to swing on a velvet rope used to section off chintz settees from the registration counter and cashier. She tried to overhear what Marc was saying as he signed them in but couldn't manage it. All her questions were answered a moment later when a bellman came around the corner pushing a luggage cart. He hesitated by her for just a moment to hand her a room key. "Your husband said you'd like a key, as well, Mrs. Elliott. I'll bring your luggage along in a moment."

"Right." Marc came up behind him. "I'll show you what we'll need. Darling, you might as well take John up to our suite," he told Dana.

Suite. The words reverberated in Dana's mind

as she stared at him. That meant more than one room and answered the question of where they were going to sleep. Or at least, offered some alternatives.

"Me go now." It was John who brought her back to the present and made her aware of Marc still waiting impatiently for her to move.

"Of course, sweetie." Dana did her best to sound maternal and she managed a little better as she smiled up at Marc, batting her eyelashes in the process. "Don't be long, darling. I've been looking forward all day to finally being able to relax with you." Her comment brought a broad grin to the face of the listening bellman and a surge of red to Marc's face.

It wasn't much of an exit line but it was the best she could manage on the spur of the moment, and Dana felt a surge of triumph as John clutched her hand and they started down the hall.

" 'Imming pool?" he asked hopefully as they passed a kidney-shaped one in the central patio.

"Maybe later, love," she told him, adding a mental note that if they did take a dip as a family before dinner, she'd make sure to stay away from the deep end if Marc were around.

Chapter Three

The phone started ringing almost as soon as Dana had finished surveying their suite. There were two bedrooms on either side of a combination television-sitting room tastefully decorated in a cool green and white. John peered into the tiny refrigerator and then asked hopefully for "Toons?" as he paused in front of the television. The first ring of the phone came when Dana was still punching the remote to find a possible station and she lifted the phone receiver casually, sure that it was probably a wrong number.

When a sultry feminine voice responded to her absent-minded "hello" with "Mrs. Elliott? This is Michelle Gonzalez," she almost dropped the receiver.

The voice went on, sounding more impatient than come-hither as she said, "This *is* Mrs. Marc Elliott, isn't it?"

"I think so" was on the tip of Dana's tongue, but she had sense enough to clamp down on the automatic response and murmur, "Yes, of course. Could you hold on just a minute, please. I have to find a cartoon program."

Fortunately, Mrs. Gonzalez figured out that Dana wasn't searching the stations for her own enjoyment. "Oh, yes. Your little boy. Marc mentioned that you'd brought him along."

By that time there was a familiar long-eared rabbit on the screen and John was already riveted to the story. Dana took a deep breath, wondering how to follow the dialogue when she hadn't even seen a copy of the script. "That's right," she said finally, aware that she must sound like a slow learner if there ever was one.

The long pause before Michelle Gonzalez continued showed that the same thought had occurred to her. "Well," she said finally, in a tone that wasn't quite as full of *joi de vivre* as before, "I just called to confirm our dinner date tonight. I'm looking forward to meeting you—unless, of course, you have trouble finding a sitter for your young man."

Dana's eyes narrowed at that. Obviously, Mrs. Gonzalez could survive very well at dinner if both Marc's wife and son were missing. Her measurements probably matched that sultry voice and her television preferences were for the late, late show.

Instead of taking the easy way out, Dana was amazed to hear herself saying, "I'm sure that Marc will arrange for a dependable sitter. He's marvelous at things like that. Actually, he's a real family man at heart."

She heard the hall door open on that last sentence and looked up to see the "family man" surveying her wryly. Dana felt her pulse accelerate and decided to retire from the field. "He's just come in," she said to Michelle. "I'll let you talk to him about the dinner arrangements." Then, covering the receiver as she shoved it toward Marc, she said in an undertone, "Here. It's Michelle Gonzalez making sure you don't miss dinner with them and checking on the window dressing. I'm going in to unpack."

A harried expression passed over Marc's face momentarily before it smoothed to his usual unflappable facade. He took the receiver and pointedly turned his back as he said, "Michelle? It's nice to talk to you again."

That was as much as Dana could hear after she'd picked up John and headed for the far bedroom.

"Dan-Dan play me. We go 'imming pool?" he wanted to know, squirming to get down.

"I'm not sure," Dana said, lowering him to the floor. "Let's find your train engines and make a tunnel here on the bed," she said, trying to sound enthusiastic. "We'll open the toy bag and get all the stuff."

Dumping the toy bag was drastic, but it held his attention for the next five minutes. When the makeshift railroad tunnel made out of a room service menu began to lose its attraction, John reverted to his familiar theme. "Me go 'imming pool," he repeated in his childish treble.

"We'll have to ask your uncle," Dana said, trying for a delaying tactic.

At that moment, the connecting door opened and Marc poked his head in. "Dinner's at eight.

I've got some things to accomplish before then, though."

"Like getting a sitter?" Dana asked, noting that his harried look had returned. "If there's a problem . . ."

"That's not what's bothering me," he said, cutting in decisively and then groaned as John ran into him at full tilt.

"Me go 'imming pool," the toddler announced to his relative, who was still bent over in pain. "Dan-Dan play me."

"I'm glad Dan-Dan's still able to move after being with you," Marc muttered. "If you try that again, it could have serious consequences for both of us."

"I can't imagine what you mean," Dana observed, trying to hide her amusement.

"And I'm a monkey's uncle," Marc responded.

"Me no monkey," John insisted, still clinging tight to his uncle's legs. "Me John. Me go—"

" 'Imming," Marc and Dana cut in simultaneously.

"My nephew has all the subtlety of a chainsaw," Marc said, turning to Dana. "Can you manage a quick dip with him?"

"It sounds fine. I gather we're not going to make it a family outing." She kept her tone light to hide her sudden disappointment.

"Not this time," he said, gently prying John's clutching fingers from his trousers. "And don't unpack any more of John's stuff than necessary. We might have another change of plan." He raked his fingers through his hair in a gesture that showed his calm demeanor was strictly on the surface. "God! I feel as if I'm trying to schedule a handful of Mexican jumping beans."

Dana opened her mouth to protest and then closed it again when Marc gave her a warning glance and steered John her way.

"This little guy isn't the Matt Biondi type, no matter what he claims. I recommend some very serious lifeguard duty."

"I hadn't planned to tell him to hold his nose and drop him off the deep end," Dana retorted.

"Good. Then I won't be forced to reciprocate with you," Marc said without missing a beat. "Have a good time in the 'imming pool, chum," he said, bending over John. "I'll see you later."

That last phrase seemed to be his theme song, Dana thought irritably as she pawed through John's suitcase to find his swim trunks. But after she had unearthed a tiny pair in pale blue, she had to laugh because John was trying to shed his clothes as fast as possible so that she wouldn't change her mind in the interim.

"Not so fast, young man," she said, reaching over to tickle his tummy. "You have to untie those shoes first before they come off. Let me help you and then you can pick out a nice rubber duck to take while I'm changing."

John grinned up at her, obviously all too willing to do anything as long as a session in the " 'imming pool" was at the end of it.

His cooperation continued once they arrived at the pool and he sat down on the edge to take off his rubber thongs. Then he stared anxiously up at Dana in her aqua bikini.

She knelt beside him and ruffled his flaxen hair. "Tell you what. Let's just sit on the steps at the shallow end until we see how cold the water is. Okay?"

He nodded and clutched her fingers with one hand while grasping a rubber tugboat with his other.

After the initial shock which made him draw in his breath, the cool water seemed to please him. Fortunately, there were only two other people in the pool—a couple who smiled at John and stayed down at the deep end as they chatted and did an occasional lap across the water.

"Would you like me to take you for a little ride?" Dana asked John once he'd gotten used to the pool by sitting on the second step leading into the shallow end. "I promise I'll hold on tight. Okay?"

At his hesitant nod, she went on briskly. "Let's put your boat on the side here and you can have it as soon as we come back."

The gentle ride went smoothly, although John's small hands clasped her forearms in a desperation grip.

"Go sit now," John said, carefully keeping his chin out of the water on the second circuit of the pool.

"Right. Back to the steps," Dana agreed, and made a gentle turn to take him back. The shadow of a tall figure at the side of the pool made her stumble over the bottom step. "What are you doing here?" was all she could manage to say as Marc casually dropped a towel on a lounger nearby and came down the steps to assist John in reaching his boat.

Dana tried not to stare, but the combination of so much tanned skin and the brief black swim trunks made her swallow inadvertently.

Apparently she hadn't been the only one doing a "once over lightly." Marc let his glance linger accusingly as he said, "If they charged by the amount of material in that outfit of yours, you must have gotten a rare bargain."

"It isn't different from any other bikini," Dana said, annoyed to find herself on the defensive again. "If you must know, I usually use it for sunbathing in my patio and I just threw it in at the last minute." She started up the steps. "Since you're here now, I can let you take over—"

Her words broke off as his hand caught her by the forearm when she tried to pass. "Don't be a damned fool," he said roughly. "There's no need to go off in a huff."

"You've made me feel as if I should audition for a part in a burlesque show." She looked down at her dripping form for confirmation. "As a matter of fact, this bikini is almost Victorian compared to some models."

"It doesn't look one bit Victorian when you're wearing it." He rubbed the back of his neck as if the muscles there were aching. "I guess I'd better apologize."

"Well . . ."

"Dan-Dan play me?" John shifted his attention from his boat to ask anxiously.

Dana smiled and sat down beside him on the step. "You have a powerful advocate here," she told Marc.

"Good. Maybe I can improve my mood by soaking my head." He gave his nephew an affectionate pat on the shoulder and pushed off toward the deep end in a powerful crawl.

Dana ostensibly kept her attention on John's tugboat, but she'd also counted six laps of the pool before Marc came back to the steps.

"Your turn now—I'll take over with the tugboat captain here," he told Dana. "That is, if you dare swim in that outfit," he added with a barest touch of a grin.

"I'll make sure that everything's still in place before I surface," she assured him and heard something that sounded like "Pity" before she, too, headed for the deep end of the pool.

It wasn't much later that she came back to the steps and said, "I'm starting to get cold," after a look at John.

Marc caught on to her diplomatic approach and stood up with the tugboat in one hand and John's wrist in the other. "So am I. We'd better go and get dressed. Incidentally," he remarked over his shoulder as he retrieved towels from the nearby lounger, "I've arranged for John's sitter tonight."

"Are you sure it's someone reliable?"

"You're beginning to sound positively maternal," he taunted, before going on in a pleasant, businesslike tone, "Absolutely reliable. John will be well taken care of. She has a special suite here in the hotel."

"That doesn't sound like an ordinary baby-sitting service."

"I told you she was something special." Marc lowered John to the ground and started putting on the pair of miniature thongs. "Now, young man, back to the room and then once you're dressed, we'll order your dinner from room service." He looked up at Dana and grinned. "What do you think? Pepperoni pizza and french fries on the side?"

"Don't give him ideas," she warned as the toddler looked up hopefully. "How about a scrambled egg and toast to compromise, with a glass of orange juice on the side?"

"Me eat now?" John was clearly torn between the swimming pool and the sound of food.

"Right. And while you're eating," Marc told him as he got into a terry cloth robe before hoisting John in his arms again, "Dan-Dan and I will have high tea or whatever passes for it in the blue grass state. Our dinner reservation isn't for a couple of hours and I'll never last without some sustenance," he explained as they made their way back into the building.

By the time Dana had showered and pulled on a coral floor-length robe, John's dinner had arrived. By then, Marc had his nephew dressed in shorts and a navy-blue T-shirt decorated with a white sailboat on the front. While John was tucking into his scrambled egg, Dana surveyed the coffee pot and lifted a silver cover to discover a trayful of cinnamon rolls. "Not a cucumber sandwich in sight," she commented to Marc.

He looked up in surprise from putting strawberry jam on John's toast. "You mean, that's what you were hoping for?"

"Only if faced with imminent starvation," she assured him, reaching for a sweet roll. "Shall I pour your coffee now?"

"Please." He seemed to be concentrating on the toast. "I'll take John up to the sitter when we're finished here. That'll give you time to get dressed. Did you bring along anything . . ." he waved the toast in a gesture that wasn't as casual as he hoped. "You know what I mean," he said finally.

"Not really. This is just a dinner date, isn't it?"

"Of course. It's just that Michelle . . ." He paused as if hunting for the right words.

"You mean Mrs. Gonzalez," Dana prompted.

"Naturally." He gave John the piece of toast, but his attention clearly wasn't on the task and Dana had to lean over and break it into more manageable pieces. Marc frowned and stared into his cup of coffee. "I meant that Michelle usually dresses to the teeth and then some. Since you didn't have much warning for this escapade, I wondered if you wanted to visit that boutique off the lobby. Naturally, I'd pick up the check as a business expense."

Dana couldn't decide whether she should be annoyed or amused and finally the latter won out. "Naturally," she said, keeping her tone serious. "And it's tempting. I've never had a man offer to pay for my clothes before. If you'd just made this offer last April after the I.R.S. had left me skint, I'd have taken you up on it in a minute."

Marc didn't appreciate her attempt at humor. "I gather that I'm being turned down."

Dana nodded and reached for a napkin to get rid of the toast crumbs on her fingers. " 'Fraid so. You've done wonders for my ego, though." When Marc remained pointedly silent, she went on lightly. "I brought along a dress that should be okay. A woman never knows when there'll be a susceptible male lingering in the lobby. Unfortunately, I haven't had a chance to use it until now."

"The dress or the 'come on'?"

"Neither one on this trip," she said, keeping a solemn tone. "There's something about a two-year-old clinging to your skirts that discourages men on the prowl. At least, that's my theory."

Marc raised an eyebrow. "Maybe the hunting will be better another time. In the meantime, if you could mop up the young man, I'll go and get the bag with his pajamas and night stuff."

His nephew didn't seem the least bit disturbed by the prospect of a different venue and it was Dana who lingered by the hall door a few minutes later to administer a hug and kiss while telling him to "be good."

"We're going to meet Michelle and George at the restaurant," Marc told her before heading toward the elevator with John. "I want to leave here in a half hour at the latest."

"I'll be ready," Dana promised. "You're sure this sitter you've lined up is reliable?"

"Just get dressed," Marc said. "John will probably be in better company than we will tonight, so stop worrying. If you keep on at this rate, you'll be claiming overtime pay for mental anguish."

Dana's only response to that was closing the door firmly. She was determined that he wouldn't be able to find any other reason for complaint and, a half hour later, she was waiting in the sitting room of their suite. Her patterned silk suit in turquoise, beige, and fuchsia had been a purchase that consumed a two-week paycheck a month earlier and she hoped that Marc thought it justified the expense. She glanced again in the mirror on her bedroom door checking that her sheer hose were the right shade with her high-heeled beige pumps and that her lipstick matched the fuchsia in the suit.

The look on Marc's face when he returned to the room and caught his first glimpse of her was all that she could have hoped even though it faded quickly. "I see that you're ready," he said, and checked his watch.

As a compliment it left a lot to be desired and any thoughts Dana might have had about telling him that his beige gabardine blazer worn with a pale blue oxford cloth shirt did terrific things for his tanned skin were put in the deep freeze.

She contented herself with saying, "Umm. Did John settle in all right with the sitter?"

"No problem." The strident peal of the telephone cut into his next sentence and he said "Damn!" as he looked at his watch again and went to answer it.

If Dana had thought his expression was irritable before, it was nothing compared to what it was after he listened to thirty seconds of the telephone conversation. "Who *is* this?" he broke in finally, and then said "God damn it to hell!" an instant later before hanging up.

"What in the world was that about?" Dana asked when he simply stayed hunched over the telephone. When he didn't answer, she went over to him and plucked at his coat sleeve. "Marc?" she asked tremulously.

He glanced around and took a deep breath. "I'm sorry. What did you say?"

"I just wondered what was wrong. Is it your brother-in-law?"

Marc brushed that aside like a troublesome gnat. "No, of course not, Look, we've a few minutes to spare. How about going down to the bar and having a drink?"

"I thought we were running close on time. That's what you said."

"So maybe I made a mistake. Frankly, I could do with something long and cool plus plenty of ice. How does that sound to you?"

Dana stared up at him, perplexed. "Whatever you say," she replied finally.

"I knew I could count on you to cooperate."

He took her elbow in a firm grip and steered her to the small bar off the lobby. After seeing her seated next to the long window which faced onto the swimming pool, he gave their order for two gin and tonics and then consulted his watch again. "I'll leave you to enjoy the scenery for a few minutes," he said, not bothering to sit down for even a token amount of time. "Hang on to my drink for me but go ahead with yours. In case I'm held up." The last remark was tossed over his shoulder as he disappeared around the corner toward the elevator.

Dana opened her mouth to protest and then closed it again when she saw that she'd be addressing an empty corner of the room. Sitting alone in a bar made her the target of several interested masculine glances, despite the two glasses ranged on the table in front of her. Probably they think I'm a two-handed drinker, she decided, trying to keep her attention strictly on the patio pool.

It was fully twenty minutes later before Marc reappeared. He looked harried and was mopping his brow with an immaculate white handkerchief when he came around the corner again. He quickly tucked that into his pocket and adopted a jovial tone as he pulled up beside her. "Enjoy your drink?" he wanted to know.

"It was fine."

He disregarded her carefully level tone and went on. "Great. Let's take off then. I called the restaurant and left a message for George and Michelle that we'd be a little late. What are you waiting for?"

Her mouth dropped open and then closed again as she got to her feet. "Are you sure you don't want a long straw?"

"What are you talking about?"

"I thought you might want a few swallows of your drink on the way to the parking lot," she told him. "Is it a habit of yours to drop off your dates in the bar? You could have parked me in the lobby or even up in our room and it would have been a hell of a lot cheaper."

"You're annoyed." He made it a statement of fact but didn't pause, leading the way to the parking lot. "I thought I'd already apologized."

"Then I must have missed that, too," she told him sweetly.

The lengthy silence that followed her remark made her wish that she'd kept quiet. Certainly Marc didn't look as if he were enjoying anything about their evening plans and if it hadn't been a childish impulse, she would have pulled up and told him to go on without her. Plus the fact that for some strange reason, she wanted to have dinner with him. Even in his present mood.

He let the silence remain until he saw her seated in the van and they were driving out of the parking lot. Then he said abruptly, "We may have a change of plans tomorrow. It looks as if our visit to Lexington may be cut short."

"Oh, I hope not. I've promised John that he'll have a pony ride at the Horse Farm. He's really excited about it."

"I know." There was resignation as well as sarcasm in Marc's tone. "It was the main thing on his mind."

"Well, if we can fit that in, I don't mind postponing some of the other things I wanted to see there. I don't think John would have much patience going through the Horse Museum—although it really sounds fascinating."

"It is."

"Then you've been there?"

He nodded. "I was up here two weeks ago." He braked as they came to a busy intersection and turned right. "The restaurant's not far from here."

That subject didn't hold as much interest for Dana as the former one. "Is there any chance that you'll be able to come with us to the Horse Farm tomorrow? At least, for part of the day?"

"Maybe." He frowned as the car in front of them changed lanes abruptly. "We'd better give that impression to the Gonzalez family tonight. Remember, this is a fun family outing."

"It would be better if you didn't say that through clenched teeth."

"If I had my choice, I wouldn't be here at all," he informed her. And then after a sideways glance at her set expression he went on hurriedly, "You needn't look as if I'd just stabbed you in the back. None of this is your fault. I'm just sorry that I ever got you involved in it."

"If I had the slightest idea what you're talking about, I wouldn't feel quite so much a third wheel."

"Maybe later," he said, slowing to pull into the curving drive leading up to a pseudo-plantation building where only a discreet brass plaque beside the door showed that it was a restaurant at all. A uniformed young man appeared like magic to open Dana's door while another was performing the same duties for Marc.

The van was whisked away and one of the men opened the ornate front door of the restaurant with a flourish.

"What do you suppose would happen if we'd appeared in a stretch limo?" Dana asked in low tones as they went into a foyer that seemed to have more marble in it than the Vatican. And then all thoughts of decorative furnishings left Dana's mind when she saw a brunette get up from a silk damask couch near the maitre d's cubicle and approach smiling.

"Marc darling," she said in throaty tones that went with her cameo-pure complexion and sleek black hair that was caught in an elegant chignon. "We were beginning to be afraid that something had happened to you." She went up on tip-toe to press a kiss that would have landed on his lips if he hadn't turned at the crucial moment so that it simply skittered along his jaw.

Dana had a mad impulse to giggle at the fleeting annoyance on the woman's face, after that. Marc gave no acknowledgment of anything untoward happening as he said calmly, "I'm sorry but I did warn you, Michelle. Darling," he said with a fond glance down at Dana, "this is Michelle Gonzalez."

"So you're the one who's finally corralled this elusive man," Michelle said, oozing charm again as she surveyed Dana. "George and I couldn't have been more surprised when he told us that he had his family along. Traveling with a toddler must be exhausting."

"John's a little young for dinner dates," Dana said diplomatically. "He's at the motel with a sitter now so we could have a night out." She tried to make her tone as pleasant as Michelle's, but it was an effort. The woman obviously would have preferred Marc without a female companion. Not that she was blatant about it. Her outfit was "jungle chic," with a linen jacket in a zebra print over black linen shorts which were just an inch or so above the knees but short enough to reveal a pair of legs that would have attracted attention anywhere. When teamed with the deep V of the jacket, most males would have been hard-pressed to know where to look first. All of it might have been on the whistle-bait borderline, but Michelle's carriage and demeanor appeared beyond reproach.

Certainly the maitre d' didn't have any doubts as he bowed and oozed a welcome, urging them to follow past a fountain to a select alcove in the corner of the room.

Marc frowned as he surveyed the empty table. "Where's George?"

Michelle made an airy gesture. "You know that husband of mine. When he heard you were delayed, he said he had some phone calls to make. I'm sure he'll be along any minute. Shall

I slide in?" Without waiting for an answer, she slid along the velvet cushion to the back of the round table, displaying an abundance of sheer black hose in the process. "Marc—why don't you sit next to me." She patted the cushion invitingly. "Then—Dana, is it?"

Just as if remembering the name was almost beyond her, Dana thought irritably as she sat next to the end of the crescent cushion.

At that moment, a thin, freckled-faced man with thick auburn hair came bustling up and slid into the banquette on the other side. "Marc— I'm sorry. Did Michelle give you my apologies?" Without pausing, he turned his attention to Dana. "And so this is your wife. I couldn't have been more surprised to hear the news."

"As you've probably gathered, darling," Marc said to Dana, "this is George Gonzalez."

"Just make it George," the newcomer said, leaning across the white tablecloth to clasp her hand. "We're delighted you could make it, aren't we, *querida*?"

Michelle gave him a smile that lasted a good two seconds before saying, "Of course. Just what I was saying to Marc before you arrived."

In another age, Dana decided they'd all have been put to the stake for telling such blatant falsehoods. It was hard not to stare at the man across the table who had just joined them. With a name like George Gonzalez, she had expected a smooth, olive-complexioned man with a thick Hispanic accent. Instead, he could have served as a model for Normal Rockwell when he painted the man next door. And the only accent she heard was a tinge of New England.

Some of her surprise must have shown in her face because Gonzalez leaned across the table and said with a laugh, "You aren't the first one to be confused, Dana. I was adopted as an infant and, from what I've been told, the doctor didn't bother to try and match up backgrounds. My poor *mamacita* spent most of her life receiving strange looks when her friends caught sight of my hair and freckles."

"From what I've heard," drawled Michelle, "it didn't bother her a bit. You were the golden boy even then."

"I'm sure that Dana isn't interested in my boyhood charm," George reproved, although he didn't look too upset by Michelle's comment.

Add a monstrous ego to the freckles, Dana thought, and started revising her ideas about the idealistic "boy next door" theme.

"I'll go along with that," Marc said, sounding more brusque than usual. "Let's order, shall we? We can't make this too late tonight. Baby-sitters make all the rules," he added in explanation. "Dana will vouch for that."

"Oh, yes," she concurred after a momentary pause. Then, determined to play her role to the hilt, she went on, "Although this one seemed more reasonable than most. I don't think she'd mind a few minutes overtime," she said, bestowing a wide-eyed look at Marc.

It obviously wasn't the right thing to say as Marc whipped his napkin into his lap with a motion that made her suspect he'd like to change it into a noose for her neck. "Well, I would," he growled. "This headache of mine is settling into a migraine. I'm sorry to be such bad company," he said to George and Michelle. "I thought the damned thing would go away after I took my usual pills but they don't seem to be working this time."

"You don't have to apologize. I've had some rotten headaches myself and it's hard to even be pleasant," George commiserated. "Do you want to try some bouillon? Or perhaps just give the whole evening a miss and go back to the motel and relax?"

"If you don't mind, I think I'll opt for the latter," Marc said, putting his napkin on the table. "There are some important questions to discuss with you tomorrow so I'd better try and get some rest tonight. We'll take a rain check on dinner and meet at your office tomorrow, if that's all right. What do you say to nine o'clock?"

"Sounds good to me," George assured him. He turned to Michelle. "Shall we stay on and have dinner? As a matter of fact, Dana might as well join us. There's no need to cancel the whole party."

Marc's eyebrows drew together but he merely said, "Of course, it's up to her."

His opaque glance didn't give anything away, but Dana suddenly felt as if she'd missed the first reel of the picture. It was strange that he hadn't said anything about a headache earlier. In fact, as he'd been churning up and down the swimming pool, he'd looked the picture of health. Admittedly, his temper had gotten progressively worse, but even so, she had no desire to share dinner with two comparative strangers. Michelle obviously wasn't keen to have her either, though if Marc had been at a loose end, the circumstances would have been different.

"What do you say, darling?" Marc's indulgent tone didn't match his intent glance.

"I think you need a private nurse," Dana said, reaching for her purse and making motions to leave. "You know that bit about 'in sickness and health.' Well, now's the time you start collecting."

"How sweet," Michelle said in a tone that didn't mean anything of the sort. "Well, at least we'll see you tomorrow, Marc."

"Of course," George agreed, getting to his feet as the waiter came rushing over when it appeared that he was losing two of his patrons. "I'll take care of things here—you two go on along."

"Right. Thanks very much," Marc said tersely as he put a firm hand in the middle of Dana's back and steered her toward the door.

Their abrupt departure caught the valet parking men unaware, but they rallied quickly and the van appeared not long after Marc had gotten a bill out of his wallet for the tip.

Dana waited until the van doors were closed and they were on their way down the curving drive before she said, "Now, maybe you can tell me what this is all about." She shot an anxious glance at his profile and went on before he could reply, "Do you really have the beginnings of a migraine?"

"No." He kept his glance straight ahead as they reached the busy roadway and made a left turn onto it, heading back toward the motel. "Something came up just before we left for dinner and the more I thought about it—it seemed like a good idea to stay on home turf."

When he didn't say any more, Dana let out an impatient sigh. "If anybody paid you by the word, they'd have a bargain. What in the dickens are you talking about?"

"I'll try to explain when we get back to the rooms." From his tone, it was evident that even though he didn't have a migraine, he regarded her questioning as a distinct pain in the neck. "In the meantime, belt up, will you? I need to think."

Dana's lips compressed in an angry tone. At least, he didn't use the excuse of traffic for staying mum. The cars had thinned out since they'd left the restaurant and it took Marc's sudden indrawn breath as he glanced at his side mirror and a violent "What the hell!" to make her clutch the edge of the seat when a delivery truck whipped by them.

The driver then cut directly in front of them, forcing Marc to brake violently and sending Dana into the dashboard as their van fishtailed onto the narrow shoulder of the highway.

As Marc brought the van to a shuddering halt off to the side of the road, she looked shakily across at him. "That idiot!" Dana could barely get the words out over the thumping of her heart. "What was he thinking of? He could have sent us all to the hospital or worse. He must have been high on something."

Marc took a deep ragged breath, "Either that or following orders." He rubbed the side of his face wearily. "At least he's gone for now. Let's get back and see if everything's all right at the motel."

"You mean John might be in danger?" Reaction made Dana's voice climb. "Oh, Lord—surely not."

Marc spared her a glance before pulling back into the lane of traffic. "I don't think we have to worry about him. He's on his way to his grandmother's house. That's what I was taking care of before we left for dinner."

Dana shook her head as she tried to assimilate everything that had happened. "And to think that I almost went abroad for a vacation because cruising around the countryside here sounded too tame."

"Before it's all over, you might wish that you had," Marc said grimly, keeping an eye on the traffic behind them. "We'll have to wait and see."

Chapter Four

When Marc let the silence lengthen between them, Dana swallowed and tried to sound matter-of-fact. "I don't know whether you're hoping to scare me to death, but I think I should tell you that you're succeeding."

"I'm not surprised." Marc kept his attention straight ahead. "That's why you'll be excused from now on—just like John."

"Hold on a minute. You're the one who signed me on for this little excursion. I think that gives me the right to decide when to quit. Besides, I want to know exactly what happened to John."

He turned his head to give her a scathing glance. "My God, you make it sound as if I'd stowed him away in a trunk."

"Now you're being ridiculous! I just don't think it was very smart to send him off with a stranger. Why on earth didn't you tell me what was happening? I could have stayed at the room and taken care of him."

"You wouldn't have a prayer. Didn't that fellow who was trying to run us off the road get through to you? They play rough here. Damned rough when it comes to threatening little kids. It was probably a bluff, but I couldn't take a chance."

"But to let him go off with a stranger—"

"He didn't."

"But you had him with a sitter."

"A special one." Marc checked the rearview mirror before turning into the parking lot alongside their motel and carefully pulled into an empty space which was well lighted.

"What do you mean by that?"

He turned off the key with a decisive motion and turned to face her, frowning. "Don't you ever stop asking questions?"

"Occasionally, when I get a plausible answer. Right now, it seems to me that you've been . . ." she paused and searched for the right words.

"Lying in my teeth," he cut in.

"You said it—I didn't."

"But that's what you were thinking."

"Exactly what I was thinking," she said, nodding.

"Okay." He rubbed the back of his neck wearily. "So maybe I left a few things out. Let's go in the coffee shop here and have a hamburger or something for dinner. After I check the rooms upstairs," he added, getting out of the van. "You can go on in if you want."

"And you'll be down in a few minutes." She shook her head. "Not again. This time I'm coming up with you."

He came around the van and closed the passenger door behind her before taking her elbow.

She pulled it away irritably. "I *do* know the way."

"I was merely trying to be polite." His eyebrows came together in a line that didn't bode well for dinner or the rest of the evening. "Did anyone ever tell you that you're damned hard to get along with?"

She pulled to a stop as they reached the door of the building and gave him a frank stare. "I'm sorry. Everything's been so confusing. Are you sure that John's all right?"

Marc gave a snort of laughter and reached around her to pull open the door of the building. "I saw him into his car seat myself."

"Yes, but to go away with a stranger—"

"He wasn't sitting with a stranger. His grandmother's taken charge and believe me, I'd rather face a pride of lions than to dally with her only grandchild."

Dana's mouth dropped open again. "His grandmother?" she said dazedly. "How in the dickens did she get here so fast?"

"Well, if you must know," he began, and then broke off to say, "I'm not going to have a confessional in the lobby of this place. Let's wait until we get up to the suite."

Dana was content to go along with that and they marched in silence to the elevator and then down the long hallway to their rooms. Marc used his key and stood aside to let her precede him into the pleasant bedroom. Or, at least it had been pleasant, Dana thought as she stopped abruptly to stare at the scene in front of her.

"I'll be damned!" Marc pulled up behind her and then slammed the hall door behind them as if venting his anger. "Whoever it was has certainly been busy tonight."

"I don't understand," Dana said, going over to inspect suitcases which had been emptied of their contents on a queen-sized bed. "We must have had a very high-class intruder."

"What do you mean?"

She gestured around the room. "Just look. Aside from my luggage, everything's still in place. If they hadn't left the desk drawers partly open, I'd never known they'd gone through them." She went over to pull open the center section. "It must be a local gang. They didn't take any of the postcards."

Marc had been rummaging through the belongings from his suitcase but he looked up to shake his head. "You're either suffering from delayed shock or you have a flaky sense of humor."

"Well, I'm going to have a worse case of shock if you don't go in that other bedroom and make sure that somebody isn't still here." She looked around for a possible weapon. "You really should take something with you."

He straightened to give her an irritated look before heading toward the other bedroom. "What do you suggest, the desk lamp? The whole idea is ridiculous. Whoever it was is long gone—I'll put money on it."

He disappeared into the other room and was back again in a minute, shaking his head. "Nothing," he told her. "It looks to me as if they just did a 'once over lightly' on our suitcases. What do you have in your hand?"

Without speaking, she extended her palm with a bright blue miniature railroad engine in it. "John's," she explained. "It was on the floor under the desk. You don't think—I mean—they couldn't have been looking for him, could they?"

"God, I don't know. Whoever called earlier mentioned that if I wanted to ensure the safety of my family, I'd better call off the investigation of the company. And it wasn't George or Michelle," he added before she could say anything. "I would have recognized their voices. At least, I think I would." He lowered himself onto the small sofa by the desk. "Right now, I wouldn't swear to anything. I *did* know I couldn't take any chances with John. Fortunately, his grandmother was already on the scene——"

"You mean, she was the sitter?" Dana asked incredulously.

He nodded and held up his hand before she could say any more. "I was in a hell of a mess. I couldn't introduce you to her because I didn't want to explain that we were registered as man and wife. It seemed necessary if George or his business partner were sniffing around, but—"

"You weren't keen on having your sister's mother-in-law know what was going on. Especially as your reasoning sounded a little thin," Dana finished for him.

"Not so thin, as it turned out. There's a lot of money involved in this investigation," Marc countered, waving his hand at the contents of their suitcases strewn around. "I wasn't taking any chances. Once I got John out of town, I knew you'd be all right if I stuck close by. What I didn't figure on was our almost being run off the road and possibly ending up in a hospital emergency room."

Dana shivered visibly. "You could have talked all night without mentioning that again. Although I suppose we should dwell on the positive aspects."

"You mean there are some?" There was a wealth of sarcasm in Marc's voice.

"Well, John's all right, isn't he?"

"I'm dead certain of that."

She grimaced. "I'm not sure I like your choice of words." Then, inexplicably, she giggled.

"I'll be damned if I can see anything funny about this whole deal," Marc said, obviously at the end of his tether.

"I can." There was still laughter in her voice. "Your trying to hoodwink John's grandmother about Mr. and Mrs. Smith registered down the hall."

"That was the worst part. I didn't register as Mr. and Mrs. Smith," he said defensively. "It had to be Mr. and Mrs. Elliott—in case Michelle came poking around. Which she probably did. I know Michelle."

Dana had a strong inclination to comment that she didn't doubt that in the least. That realization made the funny side of the situation disappear abruptly. "Well, Mr. and Mrs. Elliott then.

Which would have been embarrassing if John's grandmother learned about your sudden leap into matrimony."

"Since my family would probably have reminded me of it at every gathering for the next fifty years, I didn't see any point in advertising the fact," Marc said wryly. "If John's grandmother hadn't arrived early, there wouldn't have been any trouble."

"But as it was—"

"I'm damned glad she did," he concurred. "Although for about thirty minutes, I felt as if I were in a French farce—trying to keep you in the bar out of sight and John safely ensconced with his 'sitter' upstairs."

"You could have told me," Dana made an effort to sound matter-of-fact.

"Maybe I wasn't keen to see you breaking into hysterical laughter at that moment. The way you did a few minutes ago," Marc said with a wary look.

"I suppose you have a point," Dana agreed. "My sense of humor is a little off-beat when I'm tired or hungry. And right now—I'm both. Do you suppose we could find a room service menu in the desk drawer?"

"You're sure that's the way you want to go?"

"Well, I'm not keen about driving around the neighborhood after what happened earlier or even sitting in the coffee shop. Right now, I'd be happy to settle for a sandwich up here."

Marc went over to lift the telephone receiver

as he said, "You're getting cheated in the food line. Probably you should have stayed with George and Michelle. At least, you'd have been wined and dined in blue ribbon style."

Dana stared at him, wondering if he could be serious. He replaced the receiver and returned her glance with a level one of his own. "After thinking it over, I can't believe they would have pulled anything suspicious at the restaurant," he admitted. "They're not the kind for that. Devious, yes, but always taking care to cover their tracks."

Dana nodded slowly. "George seemed like the kind of man that a girl's parents hope she'll marry. But after meeting Michelle, I'd guess that he's not the type to hanker after his high school sweetheart. Unless she had measurements like Miss Universe and a loose set of morals." When she saw him start to grin, she tried to hide her embarrassment by saying, "Are we going to eat or just—"

"Tear Michelle to pieces," he finished for her and lifted the receiver again. "Right now, I'm a hell of a lot more interested in doing that to a turkey sandwich."

Their room service order arrived fifteen minutes later. Dana had used the interval to change into more comfortable clothes after Marc had stated his intention of doing the same thing. He was lounging in suntan cotton pants and a T-shirt that made Dana realize once again how broad his shoulders were.

His glance had gone swiftly over her multicolored caftan when she'd reappeared, but his only comment had been. "Definitely the kind for the girl next door."

It was impossible to tell if he meant it as a compliment and Dana had her doubts. She did know that Michelle's lounging outfits would be a different kind, and tried to tell herself that it didn't matter in the least. Michelle hadn't been hired as a baby-sitter. That thought made her blurt out, "I just realized that you don't need me anymore." When his eyebrows went up, she added, "Now that John isn't here, everything's changed."

Marc stared fixedly at the turkey sandwich in front of him. So fixedly that Dana asked, "Is something wrong with it? Surely you're not worried about the food here. That room service waiter was barely out of high school and I can't see him sprinkling arsenic on top of the mayonnaise."

Marc closed his eyes as if in pain. "Any more comments like that and the men in white coats will be knocking on the door." Then, he added, "I was just trying to think what tomorrow is going to bring before I drop you off at the airport with a ticket home."

Dana realized that she'd gone too far. "I'm sorry," she said, wondering about her newfound talent for alienating the man across the table. "After all that's happened, I guess I'm a little unstrung. I'm just hoping you won't—"

"Won't what?"

"Pack up my things and take me out to the airport tonight."

"That depends."

"On what?"

"Whether there are any more insinuations about arsenic in the mayonnaise. Aren't you going to eat that pickle?"

"Not if it helps my cause," she said with a grin, holding out her sandwich plate to him.

He promptly appropriated the dill slice and pretended to consider it. "Actually, it might be safer to keep you on display for a while longer. If you and John both disappear overnight, Michelle and George might start wondering." He took a swallow of iced tea and settled more comfortably in his chair. "The Horse Farm is the logical place for you to put in an appearance."

She nodded. "Apparently there are some wonderful exhibits besides all the horses on display. Unfortunately I'd already told John about the pony rides they have."

"That couldn't have helped his ride home with his grandmother. Knowing John, he probably was quoting 'Dan-Dan' and 'horsey' every five minutes."

"Maybe he forgot."

Marc's eyebrows went up again. "Sure, and maybe I'm St. Nicholas in disguise." He let out a weary sigh. "Oh, well, it can't be helped now. Maybe one day, we can make it up to him."

At his use of that all-inclusive pronoun, Dana's breathing quickened momentarily and then settled back down again. Obviously, it had merely been a slip of the tongue. A man didn't give a woman a one-way plane ticket out of town in one moment and plan future family gatherings with her in the next.

"Is there something wrong with your sandwich?" There was real concern in Marc's face as he stared at her.

She looked up to meet his glance. "Are you kidding?"

"No, I'm not kidding," he said with terrible patience. "You were looking at it as if something was crawling around in the lettuce."

Dana could hardly explain that her thoughts didn't have anything to do with the room service fare. She pushed back her plate and said, "That's my usual expression when I'm a little short on sleep. Sorry. I didn't mean to spoil your appetite."

"You didn't—oh, for God's sake!" Marc got to his feet and went over to stare down at the patio. "We'd better postpone any more discussions until morning. Maybe we can do better over breakfast." He turned to face her then, "Are you nervous about sleeping alone in your bedroom?"

If she'd had any sense, Dana would have flared back with an adamant negative, but unwillingly her mind took a tangent onto the possible alternatives. When the direction of her thoughts became evident to Marc through her suddenly flushed complexion, he let out a bark of laughter. "You can't accuse me of that. My God, you've already made it perfectly clear how you feel about me."

"I don't know what you're talking about," she countered feebly.

"Oh, come on. You practically jump a foot whenever I come near you. Not only that—" He gestured disdainfully at her voluminous caftan. "That's about as sexy as a winding sheet. Because we're alone in a room I suppose."

"You can't blame me for that," Dana responded, only aware of his final accusation. "I'd packed for this trip before I even knew that you and John were going to be a part of it. Besides, I always bring along a robe like this."

"In case of fire or room service," he said sarcastically. "I'm sure you haven't had any trouble in those categories."

By that time, Dana was so angry that she felt tears welling behind her eyelids. "You should be thankful that I'm not one of those females who's waiting to trip you at the bedroom door. I thought you'd be above such outdated comments."

"There's nothing outdated about preferring to see some chiffon and lace instead of that—that tent," he retorted, gesturing.

"Well, if I had some chiffon and lace along, I certainly wouldn't drag it out for you."

"Why not? After everything that's happened today, a little relaxation might do us both a world of good." His appraising look showed he wasn't impressed. "Now's the time for you to start retreating again—you'd better get going."

Dana pulled herself erect, doing her best to

appear unscathed by his criticism. "As you said earlier—we'll do better to talk in the morning. And no—I'm not in the least nervous about sleeping alone in my bedroom."

"In fact, the thought of any alternative arrangement would send you screaming to the hallway." His lips quirked in a crooked smile. "Keith has mentioned how you keep most of the male sex in the deep freeze."

"He had no right—"

Marc ignored that. "What in the hell are you waiting for? There aren't many Galahads riding white horses on the horizon these days."

"I don't have to explain my reasons for not playing musical beds to you or any other man," she said, more annoyed than ever.

Marc moved over to stand in front of her. "I don't advocate playing musical beds, for God's sake. These days, I can't think of a more stupid way of life. On the other hand," he reached out and pulled her up against him with a determined movement, "I don't see why I have to give up all the perks. You're still working for me. What did they used to call it . . ."

"Droit de seigneur," she said, trying to sound calm.

He nodded. "Now they'd call it sexual harassment. So maybe it would be better if I just gave you a harmless kiss good night." He let his lips move softly over her forehead before he straightened again and gave her a gentle shove toward her bedroom door. "There—no harm done. And Dana . . ."

She pulled up and glanced at him over her shoulder, trying very hard to keep her disappointment hidden. "What now?"

"If you get cold, I'm sure the housekeeper will send up another blanket."

Chapter Five

By all rights, Dana should have tossed and turned in her bed for hours after such a leavetaking. For the first fifteen minutes, she did just that—grinding her teeth at Marc's arrogance while wishing she could have put them to better use on his miserable person. That good night kiss was exactly the kind he'd bestow on John. While it might be suitable for a two-year-old, a red-blooded woman in her twenties had every right to expect a little more.

Then Dana realized that her thoughts had done an about-face somewhere along the line and she muttered a fervent "Damnation!" as she punched her pillow, which had taken on the resilience of a concrete block. It occurred to her suddenly that she hadn't even attempted to lock her bedroom door and then she remembered that it led into their common sitting room. The hall door boasted a chain and a dead bolt, she recalled, so if their earlier visitors planned to return, it wouldn't be a silent entry.

That led her thoughts back momentarily to the six-foot man in the other bedroom, who certainly had no plans for an entry—forced or otherwise. It was while she was facing that unhappy truth that she gave a weary sigh and her eyelids came down to stay.

They fluttered open again when she became aware of an insistent knocking on that same door. Dana came up on an elbow and stared around groggily, finally managing to focus on the bedside clock-radio.

Marc's voice accompanied another tattoo of knocks. "If you don't show some life in the next five seconds, I'm coming in."

She grabbed the covers as she sat bolt upright. "Don't you dare! What do you want?" The last query was pretty feeble, since even John knew that half past seven usually meant rise and shine.

Her comment didn't go unnoticed by Marc. "What in the devil do you think. If you're interested in breakfast, room service has just arrived. And if you're hoping for scrambled eggs that are still warm, I'd suggest you come out of there in the next thirty seconds."

It was closer to four minutes before Dana had found a robe and managed to rinse her face and pull a comb through her hair. As she opened the connecting door and noted Marc's immaculately dressed figure, she was glad that she'd made at least that much of an effort.

Marc's only reaction was to pull out a chair on the far side of the table with absent-minded courtesy. She waited until he'd seated himself and reached for the carafe to pour their coffee before she opened her mouth to suggest that they forget what had happened the night before.

Unfortunately, he didn't give her time to utter the first words. "I've already gotten in touch with John's grandmother and they're safely at home, so I don't think we have to worry any longer on that score. There's a plane out of here to Dallas later this morning or if you want to stay over to see the Horse Farm today, I can book you on the early flight tomorrow."

The coffee that Dana had been sipping suddenly tasted sour in her mouth. Like the old joke—"Here's your hat, what's your hurry"—it seemed that Marc had decided she'd outlived her usefulness.

"I would like to see the Horse Farm since I've come this far," she told him, trying to sound as if it really didn't matter too much one way or the other.

Marc emitted an audible sigh before reaching over to take the silver cover off his eggs and shoving a matching dish in front of her. "I thought you might, so I've made plans accordingly. There'll be a driver here at ten to take you to the Horse Farm and show you around during the day."

Dana was so surprised by his remarks that her coffee splashed on the tablecloth. "Oh, damn!" she muttered, staring at the brown stain.

"Relax." Marc reached over with an extra napkin to hide it and sat back again. "You'll live longer."

"I hate people who pontificate," she informed

him, hoping that she'd chosen the right word. "What makes you think that I need anybody to show me around? I speak the language and don't have to change my money."

"Very funny," he said in a tone that didn't mean anything of the kind. "Right now, you're still my responsibility, and somebody's going to be watching over you until I put you on a plane tomorrow."

Dana wanted to ask why he couldn't be the watchdog but didn't have the nerve. "It seems like a lot of trouble," she said finally, picking up her fork and staring down at her plate without much interest.

"You'd better eat that. Dinner was on the thin side last night and it looks as if it'll be a hot day to be traipsing around outside." He reached for a slice of toast and broke off a piece to put on some jelly. "I wouldn't try to cover everything in the Horse Park or you'll be walking on your knees by afternoon."

"The voice of experience?" she said, trying another sip of coffee.

He nodded. "I'm sorry I can't take you today, but there are some other things I have to do."

He didn't sound particularly sorry, Dana thought, keeping her glance on her plate. "Still trying to solve the mystery?"

"You might say that. I'm supposed to meet George and Michelle this morning—to hear their side of the story. If they have one."

Dana brought her gaze up then to meet his. "Won't they wonder where I am?"

"I don't see why," he retorted calmly. "Married couples don't live in each other's pockets. Naturally, I won't tell them about your leaving tomorrow."

"Naturally. Or the mad driver on the way home last night."

"You're catching on."

Dana took her coffee cup and held it between her palms, feeling an overpowering urge to dump its contents on his arrogant head. It would certainly create chaos on his immaculate white shirt and lightweight gray suit—to say nothing of his slicked-down hair that still was damp from his shower.

Some of her thoughts must have penetrated because he frowned suddenly. "I'm sorry about this. The change of plans, I mean." He threw his napkin down on the table with more force than necessary. "Everything's gone to hell!"

"It's all right," she said calmly, feeling better. "After all, nothing really happened last night and I'm wondering if the break-in here wasn't somebody looking for something hockable."

"In that case, wouldn't your jewelry be missing? I even had a little spare cash that I'd left in a coat pocket. Your run-of-the-mill sneak thief wouldn't have overlooked that."

"Hey, whose side are you on? I'm doing my best to look at the positive side of things."

He snorted. There was no other word for it, Dana decided, frowning across the table at him. Then he took a deep breath and said, "You can talk all you want, but you're not convincing me to change the plans today. You'll still have a chaperone, and that's all there is to it. I'll take care of your plane ticket for tomorrow so you won't have to worry about that."

Dana wanted to tell him that she wasn't worried about anything except the prospect of a safe, dull trip home, which was about as appealing as an unexpected trip to the dentist.

"What else is bothering you?"

Marc's terse question finally penetrated and she pushed back her chair from the table, trying to think of a reasonable answer—even if it wasn't the right one. "I was wondering what to wear today," she managed. "I didn't plan on mingling with the horsey set when I left home."

"You'll be mingling with more tourists than horses. There is a difference," Marc said drily, getting up and rescuing the coffee carafe and his cup before pushing the breakfast table out into the hall to be collected. "By the way . . ." His words caught her just as she was retreating into her bedroom.

She looked back inquiringly.

"I just wanted to say thanks for taking everything so well." His voice was brusque and he seemed to have trouble holding her glance.

She shrugged, determined not to let him know how close she was to dissolving into tears. "No problem. Are we going to have dinner together?" Even the most casual acquaintance was entitled to ask that, she thought.

Marc rubbed the side of his nose as he said slowly, "I don't know. I'll leave word at the desk if I can't make it. In the meantime, wait up here until your driver arrives. He should be here in half an hour, so you'd better get ready."

With that terse comment, he went into his bedroom, closing the door firmly behind him. After a second or two, Dana followed suit in her room, but when she'd closed the door she turned around and put her forehead against the cool surface, trying to get her emotions back in order.

The tears which streamed down her cheeks wouldn't be denied and she headed doggedly for the bathroom to turn on the shower, determined that enough cold water would shock her back into a sensible frame of mind. Her only consolation was the fact that Marc had no idea how his "Here's your hat, what's your hurry" plan had hurt.

When a phone call from the lobby came a prompt half hour later saying that her car and driver were ready, Dana cast a quick glance at herself in the mirror over the desk and announced that she'd be right down. Her reflection showed a woman neatly dressed in a tobacco-brown cotton dress with a pleated skirt and sleeveless top which featured a flattering portrait collar. A single strand of freshwater pearls was her only jewelry since the hot weather discouraged anything heavier. She'd pulled her hair back in a mock-chignon fastened with a tangerine chiffon scarf. Peering closer, she was relieved to note that there weren't any signs of tears, although there were dark shadows which testified that some extra sleep wouldn't go amiss.

For a moment, she considered applying a little more makeup as a remedy and then shook her head irritably. The horses wouldn't care how she looked and they were the only ones going to get her attention for the next eight hours.

She didn't even hesitate as she passed Marc's bedroom door, knowing full well that he was already out of the building.

Her driver turned out to be a man in his early forties who looked as if he could have played on the defensive line of any NFL team. His hair was thinning, but that was the only thin part of him since his collar looked like the Jolly Green Giant's and seemed to meld into shoulders that were beyond belief. It turned out that his name was Harry Sinclair. His ears showed red when he introduced himself and mentioned that he was a former employee of Marc's. "Security guard," he confessed in a gravelly voice. "Then I got a chance to start my own company along the same lines, and Marc furnished part of the capital. Ordinarily I don't get out of the office much these days, but Marc said you were something special and he wanted to make sure that nothing happened to you."

The last came out in an embarrassed rush and had Dana staring at him in amazement. "How nice," she said finally, thinking that Marc had given Harry an exaggerated idea of her importance in the scheme of things. Certainly different than he'd admitted to her at breakfast.

Harry seemed puzzled by her frowning silence

and hovered by his nondescript sedan, "Maybe you'd like to sit in the back," he said.

"Heavens no." She gestured toward the front seat. "I'm glad to have a guide for the day," she went on, trying to sound as if she meant it. "You must know all about the local points of interest."

"I don't know much about horses except the betting window at the racetrack where I usually lose my money." He pulled the door open on the passenger side with a force that had her wincing for the hinges. "Maybe we can learn together at this place."

Even with Harry's bulk beside her, Dana found herself looking nervously at the cars which passed them on the busy highway. When she saw his puzzled looks, she smiled weakly and said, "Sorry. I should have mentioned that I'm sort of a backseat driver."

"That's okay. Marc told me you had a little trouble last night with somebody trying to run you off the road. I'm keeping my eyes open."

"Great." Relieved that she didn't have to indulge in any more subterfuge, Dana sat back in her seat and was able to enjoy the green grass and neat fences the state was famous for on either side of the car. It wasn't long before they turned in a drive and drove slowly up to a big parking lot where already rows of cars and several tour buses were parked.

"We're not the only ones with this idea," Dana said ruefully as she surveyed them.

"It's okay. There are a lot of acres in this place so we're not apt to be crowded." Harry pulled into an empty space and turned off the ignition. "Better take your sunglasses, the sun's strong already. It's supposed to be really hot later on."

"It's hot now," she told him with a smile. "I'm just trying to pretend that it's not. Maybe there are some horses in the shade—not like those." She gestured toward a big pasture at the end of the lot where several horses were grazing in bright sunshine near the fence.

"We'll hope so." Harry took off his jacket and tossed it on the back seat, revealing broad shoulders in a short-sleeved sport shirt that strained at the seams. "Marc arranged for our tickets— we just have to pick them up at the admission window in that building over there." He pointed toward a nearby building where groups of people were heading, obviously intent on the same thing.

The Horse Farm turned out to be a wondrous place and, while it would have been more fun if Marc had been enjoying it with her, Harry couldn't be faulted. They "pooled their ignorance," as he said, and wandered the extensive grounds. After going through the barns where the various breeds of horses were pictured and explained, they finally took a breather on metal bleachers and watched an exhibition of various breeds ridden in the ring. That meant displays of horsemanship both in the saddle and driving behind sulkies, as well.

Afterward, as they strolled up to see the Exhibition of Champions atop a rolling hill, Dana sighed. "I didn't know there was so much to

learn. You really need to do your homework before you come. Either that or allot a week to
cover everything."

Harry nodded, reading the day's program as
they went along the sunny path. "I'd do better
if we had something to eat. Are you ready for a
late lunch?"

"Definitely." She peered ahead to the small
building containing some of the legendary winners from the past. "Maybe we can just peer in
the stables here and not wait for the show. I'm
sure the horses would understand."

"Sounds good to me." Harry gestured over his
shoulder. "There's an eating place on the grounds."

She looked up at him hopefully. "Nearby?"

He shook his head. "At the other end of the
place."

"That follows." She let out an audible sigh and
quickened her pace. "Well, at least we'll have an
appetite when we get there. It's too bad that the
owners didn't include a moving sidewalk when
they drew up the plans."

"Either that, or furnish a horse-drawn carriage
for every visitor." Harry pulled a handkerchief
from his trouser pocket and mopped his ruddy
cheeks. "Okay, a quick look at the winners and
then we head for lunch and a gallon of iced tea."

It was a late lunch when they finally reached
the building housing the cafeteria. Fortunately,
there were still crisp-looking chef's salads and
the iced tea that Harry had hoped for. That thirst-
quencher seemed more satisfying than anything
else, and Dana eased her shoes halfway off while

they made their plans for the rest of the afternoon.

"There are a couple of film showings," Harry said hopefully as they discussed possibilities.

"Is it the subject matter or the fact that we'd be sitting down that sounds attractive?"

"Now you're sounding like my wife," he told her.

"I didn't know you were married," Dana said. "Is she here in Lexington, too?"

He shook his head. "We live in Dallas. Marc just brought me up here on a special assignment."

"Then you do a lot of work for him?" Dana probed.

Harry took another swallow of iced tea and grinned at her. "You could say that. I've worked with his clients for about five years now."

Dana shrugged. "He didn't tell me. Just that you were going to make sure that I didn't do anything stupid today."

"Those weren't exactly my marching orders. Marc was pretty explicit that you were to be returned to him in mint condition. I don't know when I've seen him so adamant on a subject."

"Really." Dana made no attempt to hide her pleasure at that declaration. "Then I'd better make sure that I follow orders."

"We'd both better go along with his rules." Harry put his napkin down and got to his feet. "I've gotten used to eating regularly. What's next on your agenda?"

"I'll have to admit that the spirit's willing but the flesh is getting pretty weak," she confessed.

"I would like to see the museum here before we leave, though. I've heard that it's really first rate."

"Right. It's not far away. There's a gift shop there, too. In case you're interested," he added with a crooked grin.

"There speaks the married man who understands women," she replied, standing up beside him. "I promise not to spend more than ten minutes there as a last hurrah."

"That doesn't sound like the typical feminine response," he told her. "I've also been married long enough to know that."

"It's a typical response considering the state of my checking account at the moment."

"Cash-flow problem?"

"Exactly. It's all flowing out at the moment, until I get home and have another salary check."

He reached for his wallet. "If you're serious—I could help—"

"Heavens no!" She put a hand on his arm to stop him. "I'm really doing fine, but I just plan to stay that way. That doesn't mean that I won't go through the postcard rack. This has been a wonderful day and I certainly want some souvenirs."

By then, they were on the pleasant, winding path leading back to the admissions building and just beyond, the big structure that housed the museum.

"I should check in with Marc about this time," Harry said, glancing at his watch. "There should be some public phones here." He gestured toward the admissions building. "I noticed them when we came in."

"I might as well go on to the museum," Dana told him.

"I'm not sure that's such a good idea," Harry remonstrated.

"Oh, heavens, why not? It's a beautiful afternoon with birds singing," she protested, gesturing toward some flying overhead to disappear in the shade trees alongside the path. "I think Marc was overreacting when he made you chaperone me. A waste of expensive talent," she added with a mischievous smile. "I promise not to try and pick up anybody while you're making your phone call."

"You'll be in the museum?" Harry didn't respond to her lighthearted air.

"Right on the main drag," she assured him. "And after that final bit of culture, I'll let you take me back to the motel. By then, the swimming pool will be looking very good."

Harry nodded, but was still waiting outside the main entrance when Dana looked over her shoulder before going into the museum.

There was a brightly lighted gift shop to her left, according to the signs, but she ignored that to head into the museum itself and found herself at the base of an immense spiraling ramp which was illuminated mainly by the glass-fronted displays on either side of it.

It was impossible not to be impressed by the tremendous attention to detail involving human involvement with the horse starting ten million years ago. The designers had made sure that the displays were beautifully done—showing the Greeks' part in the chronological pattern and then the development of the horse in the New World.

Dana moved on slowly, completely fascinated by the panoramas. She was viewing the "golden age" of the late nineteenth century when she felt an uneasy niggling that she was being observed.

The lighting on the ramp was purposely subdued so the displays would be even more effective. When she glanced casually over her shoulder she caught the outline of a shadowy figure standing motionless some twenty-five feet away.

Afterward, Dana couldn't recall what made a shiver of apprehension go over her on viewing that still figure. Possibly because of his stance—a crouched silhouette far different from the noisy family groups she'd seen earlier on the ramp with children clinging to rails as they asked questions or pressing their noses against the glass to view the fascinating displays.

She took another surreptitious look from the corner of her eye as she peered down the ramp, hoping to give the impression that she was looking for a friend to catch up with her. Unfortunately, there was no sign of Harry, but the waiting figure appeared to have quietly closed some of the gap.

Dana turned quickly on her heel, aware that not only was Harry among the missing—apparently all of the other paying customers were, as well. She continued at a brisk walk up the ramp and could have shouted with relief when she turned a corner and found a couple with two toddlers staring at a Civil War display case. The toddlers' obviously had a short attention span and wanted to play tag rather than wait while their parents read about the fascinating history on view.

"Isn't this wonderful!" Dana enthused, moving as close as she could into the family group. "I don't know when I've seen more attractive exhibits. Even your children seem to be thrilled." She crossed her fingers at the last since the children in question were running in circles on the ramp.

The young mother stared at Dana as if she were out of her mind before trying to quell the pair who had progressed to rolling on the floor. "Richie—stop that! Monica! Don't you dare bite him again!"

"Do what your mother says," their father ordered, reluctantly switching his attention from a McClellan saddle in the display case.

Dana quickly glanced over her shoulder again to see the shadowy figure hovering nearby and she drew an agitated breath. Surely, she'd be safe if she stayed with people around her.

The toddlers had been hauled to their feet by that time and their mother was saying distractedly to her husband, "We'll have to get them home or there'll be no living with them tonight. I told you what would happen if they missed their naps."

"But this stuff is fascinating—" he started to

protest, and then shrugged as his wife gave him a speaking glance.

As he reached down to hoist the little boy on his shoulders, Dana looked around in desperation. She couldn't very well go arm in arm with them, and they clearly weren't in the mood for conversation with a stranger. All she could do was try and stay on their heels until they reached another part of the museum where there were other people.

As they started off and Dana fell in close behind, the husband gave her the same kind of suspicious look that she had been bestowing on the silent figure. Oh, God, she thought miserably, trying to think of a possible excuse for staying practically in their pockets.

At that moment, she heard the sound of running feet behind her and turned an agonized face to confront this newest development. She opened her mouth to scream when she recognized Harry's welcome bulk hurrying up the ramp.

"Thank the Lord," she muttered as he reached her side. "Let's get out of here!"

After one glimpse at her pale face, Harry didn't argue. He caught her elbow in a possessive grasp and headed toward the nearest exit. Dana heard the couple she'd been shadowing break into excited conversation as they left and realized she'd probably be their main topic on the way home.

They were close to the bottom of the ramp and in sight of the popular gift shop before Harry pulled to a stop, still keeping a hold on her arm.

"Okay, now what's it all about? I thought you were going to faint on me back there."

"I'd have been more apt to go into hysterics," she confessed.

"But why?"

"There was somebody standing in the shadows," she began, and then seeing a frown come over his face she realized how thin her explanation sounded. "I know it sounds as if I'm going 'round the bend, but he definitely wasn't paying any attention to the displays. I was being watched, I tell you." She glanced earnestly up at him. "You must have gone past him on the ramp. Don't you remember?"

"Hell—all I remember was the terrified look on your face. And there were some kids around."

She nodded. "And their mother and father, who are probably reporting me to the security forces right now. I was sticking to them like glue—it seemed safer that way."

"No matter what the reason—you did the right thing," he told her. "I could go back up there, but I don't know exactly who I'd be looking for."

"I don't either," Dana confessed wearily. "Frankly, I'd just as soon you didn't get out of my sight. Let's go back to the motel." Her lips twisted cynically as they started walking again. "Unless there are at least five or six people around, I'm not even going in the deep end of the swimming pool."

Harry nodded in agreement. "Don't worry. I'll stick close until Marc gets back on the scene. I gather that you don't want to stop in the gift shop." He jerked his head toward the entrance on their right.

"No, thanks. Right now, all I want to do is go out in the sunshine and fresh air."

Harry smiled sympathetically. "Okay. I could do with a little less sunshine, but at least we can turn on the air conditioning when we get in the car." As they walked along, he added in a casual tone, "Can you remember anything that would help identify that man on the ramp?"

Dana stared down at the path as she tried to remember. Finally, regretfully, she shook her head. "I'm sorry. Nothing I can really put a finger on. He was just so ominous—lurking in the shadows. And so different from all the other people I'd seen on the ramp. Probably, it was just my imagination."

"I'm inclined to believe you." He sighed as they turned toward the big parking area where they'd left their car earlier. "Unfortunately, it won't go down very well on my report. I shouldn't have left you for that phone call."

"I was the one who insisted that I'd be perfectly all right in the museum. That's what I'll tell Marc, so don't worry."

"I wasn't concerned about a dressing down from him. I should have followed my own rules." He gave her a rueful grin. "You're entirely too persuasive. Marc warned me about that, too."

Dana couldn't suppress the irritation she felt on hearing that. "I'm surprised that he didn't include what cereal I like for breakfast. Are you sure that he skipped anything?"

Harry refused to rise to her bad temper. "I got the feeling that he'd like to learn a lot more about you, but, of course, you know what they say about an observer."

"Someone who sees most of the game?"

He pulled up beside their car and stooped to unlock the door. "You know more about that than I do. Anyhow, there's no use dwelling on it. If there was someone tailing you in the museum, he didn't score. Which only leaves tonight at the motel."

"And I'll think about that later." A blast of hot air from the closed car made her hesitate before getting in the front seat. "Wow! It's stifling in there. I'm glad I'm not wearing shorts or I'd be burned on that leather cushion."

"Hang on a minute until I get the air conditioning going," Harry said, going around to the driver's side. "I'm going to deliver you back in good condition one way or another."

Once they arrived back at the motel, Dana insisted on his coming up to the suite when he announced that he'd stick around to keep an eye on her.

When he started to protest, she firmly cut him short. "For heaven's sake—you're not going to lurk in the hallway. You can wait in the sitting room while I change into a swim suit and then keep tabs on me under an umbrella table at the poolside." She ushered him into the middle room of the suite. "It's too bad that you can't cool off in the pool—"

"That definitely wouldn't look right on my report," he said, cutting her off. "Drinking a gallon of iced tea on the edge of the pool can't be faulted, though. Do you want me to check out your bedroom?" he asked as she hesitated by the door.

"I'm not letting my imagination run completely rampant," she said, giving the tidy room a quick once-over and then smiling reassuringly at him over her shoulder. "I don't have to worry about anybody lurking under the beds—they'd have to be midgets to get under there."

"I see what you mean," Harry said, with a satisfied look around. "I'll check in with my office again while I'm waiting."

It didn't take Dana long to pull her bikini from her suitcase and start shedding her clothes. Despite Marc's comments, the bikini was fairly modest by St. Tropez standards, she decided, so it wouldn't shock any Lexington citizens. Especially when she donned the thigh-length print cover-up that could do double duty as a brunch coat if needed. She was thinking about that pleasing possibility when she heard another masculine voice besides Harry's in the sitting room.

As always, her pulse rate bounded and a quick glance into the mirror on the closet door showed a silly smile on her face as well as heightened color. She couldn't do much about her flushed cheeks, but she did manage to subdue the grin and take a deep breath before opening the sitting room door.

Afterward, she was glad that she hadn't lingered any longer over her appearance since Marc had the hall door open and was hovering on the threshold. When she appeared, he gave her a brief, almost stricken glance and turned back to Harry. "Maybe you'd be kind enough to wait outside," he told the husky security guard. "This won't take long. I'm cutting it fine already."

Which made it sound as if an interval with her was certainly far down on his list of priorities, Dana thought with some bitterness. "I wouldn't want to hold you up," she assured him when he'd closed the door behind Harry and turned back to face her.

"You're not going to." The comment was almost absent-minded as he shot a glance at his watch. "If I hit too much traffic, I'm in trouble as it is. Harry's going to keep an eye on you and make sure that you get safely on the plane tomorrow."

"You mean you're not coming back tonight?" There was more concern than Dana wanted in her words.

It must have gotten through Marc's preoccupation, because his expression softened for an instant as he shook his head. His voice, however, was matter-of-fact. "I'm afraid not. Recent developments have made me change my plans for the evening."

Which could mean that Michelle wasn't going to miss another dinner with him, Dana thought. The fact that he wasn't explaining his changed plans made it almost a certainty.

"Harry said that you had an unpleasant incident at the Horse Farm today. I'm sorry about that, but from now on—you shouldn't have to worry."

"How nice." Dana made no effort to hide her annoyance. "Convenient for you, too. Heaven knows how we would have passed the time if you'd had to hang around here with me tonight."

"Isn't that a fact." Marc looked at her then, as if aware for the first time of the brevity of her bikini and the amount of sleek skin on view. "Now we'll never know whether we'd have ended up playing double solitaire or . . ." He advanced and hooked a strong arm around her while his other hand moved impatiently under the cover-up to rest possessively on her hips.

Dana was so surprised that she had to swallow before she could get out a response. "Or what?"

"A different kind of game entirely," he growled, and brought his head down to kiss her demandingly.

It seemed to last forever; at least long enough for Dana's bones to melt against him while her arms found their way up around his neck of their own volition.

The need to breathe again was the thing that finally forced them apart, and Dana clung like a limpet to Marc's shirtfront listening to his heartbeat pounding in her ear as she tried to steady her own pulse rate.

She felt Marc's hands move—was it reluctantly?—as he pushed her away to a safe distance. They tightened momentarily when she swayed before she made a determined effort to regain her poise and balance. "It's a good thing

I'm going," he said then, almost bitterly. "Otherwise Keith would be waiting at the airport with a shotgun."

"I don't know what the deuce my brother has to do with anything," she said, frowning at his concern.

"He also happens to be my business partner."

"Oh, I see. And you never mix business and pleasure." Sudden anger made her voice rise. "Presuming that you found any pleasure in your—experiment." Her voice set the last word apart. "You shouldn't take things so seriously. I thought it was just a perk of my job. To make up for my minimum wage and getting fired without notice."

His sardonic look showed what he thought of that. "If I'd known you wanted extra benefits, you should have told me earlier. Anyhow, it's too late now," he informed her before turning toward the hall. "I'll see you back in Dallas when I have more time."

"I'll try to fit you in," she responded, determined to be just as nasty as possible.

That absurd comment made him hesitate after he'd opened the hall door, and he bestowed a glance that would have shriveled most people. "Don't go out of your way."

Dana was determined to have the last word but, at that moment, she couldn't think of anything adequately damning. As a result, she simply stood there—glaring.

Evidently it had some effect, because Marc's hand dropped from the doorknob and he strode back to yank her into his arms again, kissing her so hard that it was almost painful. Then he pushed her away, saying ruefully, "Hell! I must be out of my mind. Now do what Harry says until you're on that airplane." He hesitated by the hall door just long enough to add, "And make damned sure that you keep that cover-up on when you're not in the pool."

The door closed behind him with a slam that must have been heard all the way to the elevator. Dana stared at the empty hall for an instant as she rubbed the back of her hand against her bruised lips. Then a furtive smile lightened her expression as she went over to check her appearance in the full-length mirror on the closet door. There wasn't anything drastically wrong, she decided, although her cover-up had come adrift during that last embrace. Her smile broadened as she thought about Marc's reaction and she pulled her bikini top firmly back in place once again.

As her mind went over Marc's last comments, the flush that was evident on her cheeks seemed to slither all the way down to her toes. What a good thing she was heading for the pool, she decided. It was either that or a very cold shower.

Chapter Six

Any euphoria that Dana might have felt after Marc's farewell wasn't allowed to last long.

It was after she'd enjoyed a cooling swim and was toweling herself on the edge of the pool that she asked Harry what time it was. When he checked his watch and told her, she managed a casual tone for her next question.

"Did Marc say when he'd be checking back with you?"

Harry frowned, "I don't expect to hear from him again until he finally arrives back in Dallas."

"Dallas?" Dana's voice went up in surprise. "You mean he's on his way to Dallas tonight?"

"Not unless he's changed his plans at the last minute. He's en route to San Juan." Harry looked around to make sure that they couldn't be overheard by the foursome on the other side of the pool. "That's not to be noised around, though."

Dana was still staring at him. "San Juan? Which San Juan? Is there one around here?"

"Not that I've heard of. I'm talking about Puerto Rico."

That time her voice scaled another octave. "Puerto Rico! Are you kidding?"

"Calm down, for Pete's sake." Harry didn't try to hide his displeasure. "He's keeping it under wraps. Probably that's why he didn't tell you. I know he wants you out of any trouble as soon as possible. If there'd been a flight with decent connections, he would have made sure you were back in Dallas tonight."

"You make me sound like a bubonic plague carrier," she said, pulling her cover-up over her still-damp body.

Harry shook his head. "He's just trying to protect you. As a matter of fact, I wanted him to take me with him. It seems to me that he could use a little muscle in San Juan."

Dana almost dropped the towel that she was taking over to the receptacle. "You mean he's in danger down there?"

"God, I don't know." Impatience finally won out over diplomacy in Harry's voice. "He'd probably fire me for talking as much as I have." He looked around and noted two family groups who were invading the shallow end of the pool like lemmings heading for the sea. "What do you say we get out of here?"

Dana nodded, still concerned that Marc had apparently taken all the risks just to make sure that she was properly chaperoned.

"Do you want to eat downstairs tonight or have room service?" Harry was asking.

"Maybe it would be better to stay in the room rather than advertise the fact that you and I are apparently going steady," she said as he held a heavy glass door for her which led into the Jacuzzi spa area and then on into the corridor.

"Whatever you say," Harry agreed. He took time to pull a handkerchief from his back pocket and mop his forehead. "Just so there's air conditioning and you stay within sight."

"I won't quarrel with that," Dana assured him as they headed for the elevator. "I'm still too warm even in this damp swim suit."

They were still discussing the weather in desultory fashion when the elevator doors opened on their floor and they found themselves face-to-face with Michelle Gonzalez.

"What luck!" she trilled. "I was about to give up after pounding on your door." Peering around them, she frowned prettily. "But where's Marc? Don't tell me that he's going to stand me up for our cocktail date?"

Dana chewed on her lower lip as she tried to think. "I'm afraid you must have gotten your time's mixed. Marc's been called away for the moment, but he didn't say anything about getting together."

"I can't understand that. He's certainly never made that kind of mistake before," Michelle said, smoothing the side of her black and gold printed silk shorts which allowed her tanned legs to show to advantage. A matching halter top provided the same service for her elegant shoulders. She idly twisted her sunglass frame as she stared up at Harry, who stood beside Dana. "I'm sorry," she said then. "I didn't realize you were together—instead of just sharing an elevator."

"No, it's my fault," Dana said with a strained smile. "Michelle Gonzalez—Harry Sinclair. Harry's an old friend of the family who's taken pity on me today since Marc's been so busy."

"It wasn't any problem as far as I was concerned," he told her in his deep voice.

"But that doesn't really solve my problem, does it?" Michelle managed a wry pout.

"What problem is that?" Dana asked, wondering how much longer the cat and mouse game was going to go on.

"The fact that I've apparently been stood up on our cocktail date." She paused, obviously expecting Harry to hurriedly suggest that they make it a threesome down at the bar in the lobby.

Instead, he merely frowned and said, "Marc doesn't usually make a mistake like that. Dana, you'd better go on in and change before you start turning blue here in the corridor."

"It is a little chilly under the air-conditioning ducts here in the hallway. I'm sorry about the mixup, Mrs. Gonzalez. Perhaps we can all take a raincheck on it soon." Dana hoped that she sounded properly regretful as she took her leave, closing the door firmly behind her.

She headed for the bathroom and then stopped, remembering that Harry didn't have a key to the room. At least as far as she knew. Certainly he wouldn't be using one under Michelle's eagle eye. It was best to wait and see what happened.

It didn't take long. She heard a key inserted in the sitting room door and then Harry's voice saying hesitantly, "Dana? Everything okay in here?"

"Fine." She moved over to her bedroom doorway to reassure him. "I didn't want to get in the shower until I knew you had a room key."

"Thanks," he said with a brief nod. "I thought I'd better see Mrs. Gonzalez off the premises."

"I'm surprised that she let you go." Dana managed a wry smile. "It must be about the first time in history that any man got away from her clutches."

Harry merely grinned and went over to the tiny refrigerator. "Marc said there was some beer in here. Does it interest you?"

"Not at the moment, thanks. Maybe after I've showered and changed. You might check the room service menu, too. Somehow I'm in the mood to pig out."

"You'll feel better after you've had some food."

Dana nodded, subduing an impulse to tell him that calories weren't going to replace Marc. She walked back into her bedroom and, after pulling a clean pair of slacks and a T-shirt from her suitcase, headed for the shower.

The warm water helped a little bit—so did knowing that she at least was clean and scrubbed when she looked in the mirror the next time. Her hair was still damp, but she contented herself with tying it back from her face with a silk scarf before going out to the sitting room again.

Harry handed over the room service menu,

saying, "How about something long and tall to go with it? There's some gin and tonic water over there in the bar if it appeals."

Dana nodded. "Only if there are plenty of ice cubes to go in it. Have you decided what you want to eat?"

"I was waiting for you before phoning down," he said, moving over to open the small refrigerated bar. "Actually, I stopped reading when I came to a New York steak."

"Two great minds with but one single thought," Dana said, putting the menu back on the desk. "I'll phone while you tend bar. How do you like it? The steak, I mean."

"Medium is usually safest." Harry brought her drink over along with a bag of potato chips by the time she'd finished calling. "You're a good sport about all this."

"One thing you learn about traveling with Marc: be prepared for the unexpected because that's what you'll get." She waited until he'd gone back and retrieved his beer before raising her glass in a silent toast.

Harry settled his bulk on the small divan against the wall and pulled his bag of chips within reach. "He's not usually this—"

As he searched for the words, Dana broke in. "Abrupt? Pigheaded? Stubborn? Pick one."

"Let's just say he's usually more diplomatic," Harry said with a slow grin. "And, to be fair, he's not usually this pressed for time. It was necessary that he get down to San Juan as fast as possible, I gathered."

Dana took a sip of her drink. "Is it permissible to ask why?"

Harry frowned before saying reluctantly, "I don't see why not. George has apparently flown the coop. Marc thinks he's stopping over in San Juan before heading to South America and out of reach. At least as far as extradition goes. Marc can alert the authorities in Puerto Rico, plus being on hand to provide positive identification and swearing out the necessary papers."

Dana stared across at him in bewilderment. "You found all this out from Michelle?"

George's hand paused in the process of reaching for another potato chip. "Hell, no. Sorry, I didn't mean to—"

"I have heard the word before," Dana said, secretly amused at his embarrassed expression. "Well, if it wasn't Michelle, who was it?"

"Marc. He told me most of it when he was leaving. Along with instructions about watching over you."

Dana ignored the last part, wondering why Marc couldn't have taken her into his confidence, as well. Almost absently, she said, "It sounds to me as if he's the one who needs looking after."

"I brought that up, too, but I didn't get far. At least, he's being sensible about staying away from the fashionable beach area and heading for Old San Juan instead." Reaching for another chip, he said casually, "I suppose you've been there."

"A million years ago. I'm sure the whole place is different now."

Harry nodded agreement. "Especially with so many cruise boats docking there in season. They're needed to help the economy but there are still lots of things worth seeing off the tourist trail."

"Does Old San Juan rank as a good place to stay?"

She kept her voice casual but Harry's eyes narrowed as he looked across at her. "It depends. What did you have in mind?"

"Heavens, I don't know. Living in Texas, it's an easy hop to Puerto Rico. I was just thinking that next year I might head south for a vacation. Maybe go on to Grand Cayman afterward." She noted that Harry's frown disappeared as she rambled on and decided to change the subject to be doubly safe. "I wish that I'd thought to order some dessert, too. Steak sounds fine, but I'm sure I'll be hungry afterward."

Harry was apparently willing to be diverted. "We can see how we feel. Room service doesn't close until late, so you can always change your mind and call for some extra calories."

After that, the rest of the evening was smooth sailing. Dana even was methodical enough to finish her packing before going to bed, just leaving out a divided skirt of pale blue chambray with a matching blouse which was good for traveling.

The next morning—as they had arranged the night before—room service provided breakfast in the sitting room after Harry checked out the waiter. Dana decided that her bodyguard must have had a razor tucked away because he was clean-shaven and his hair showed evidence of a recent shower, though his shirt didn't look quite as unwrinkled as the day before.

He gave a wry smile when he saw her glance going over him. "I hadn't planned on twenty-four-hour duty when I started yesterday."

"You'll have to charge Marc double," Dana told him. "I hope that you got a little sleep."

"I'm in good shape, or at least I will be when I get a change of clothes." He glanced at his watch. "We'd better keep moving. I've already settled with the desk, so we won't have to hang around checking out."

"Something makes me think that you've already checked with the airport, too," Dana said, reaching for the last piece of toast on her plate.

"You're right—and your flight's on time."

"Miracles will never cease," she said lightly, finishing her coffee. " 'God's in his heaven and all's right with the world.' Did I get that right?"

Harry stood up and moved her luggage to the door. "Close enough. Want to take a last look around?"

"No, thanks." Dana hid a grin. Harry was carefully polite, but she had the feeling that only a tornado or major earthquake would keep him from putting her on that plane.

Fortunately for all concerned, no natural disasters occurred and Dana's trip back to Dallas was uneventful. She found that the airport shuttle at DFW was even faster than usual in getting her back to her apartment, and emitted a sigh of relief when she arrived.

The air conditioner was humming briskly, but she opened the balcony door to let a little fresh air in while she went over to her desk in the study and put in a call to her travel agent. After a ten-minute conversation, she thanked her and then called her brother's office number. His secretary put her through promptly.

"Hi, sis. Marc said you'd be back in town today," he said cheerfully. "How was the flight?"

"Fine. You'll be glad to know that the Cordon Bleu chefs around the world don't have to worry about any competition at thirty-seven thousand feet."

"That bad?"

"Not really. I guess I'm just a little tired." She did her best to sound as if a long nap was all that she had in mind.

"I was going to invite you over to dinner."

"Let me take a raincheck on it, will you Keith? Oh, before I forget, I have some information that Marc wanted me to get, but I'm not sure that I copied his telephone number in San Juan correctly."

"You can tell me. I'll be in touch with him soon—"

"It's no trouble." Dana cut him off ruthlessly in mid-sentence since she had no intention of letting him upset her plans. She ploughed ahead calmly, trying to sound casual. "He said it was

area code 809 and then I have 421 ..." She
paused as if checking out her number.

Just as she hoped, Keith broke in and finished
for her. "1652. I'm pretty sure that's the Re-
forma's number."

"Right. That's it. Only one more thing. Has he
registered under his name?"

"I think so. Why wouldn't he?" There was
definite suspicion in her brother's voice by then.

"Just that Harry was worried about his going
down there alone."

"Well, I wasn't too happy about it myself, but
Marc knows how to take care of himself and nobody will be looking for him in the old part of
town. It's pretty well known that he usually
stays out at the beach."

"Okay, then. I'll give him your regards. See
you later when I've caught up on my sleep."

Without giving Keith a chance to prolong the
conversation, she put the receiver down quickly
and then sat for a minute or so staring at it. She
hadn't liked to tell an out and out lie, but she
knew very well that if she'd told her brother
her plans, he would have been adamant in his
objections.

As it was, she'd call him when she arrived in
San Juan and was safely registered in the hotel
where Marc was staying. The travel agent had
given her the name of two or three possible hotels in the old section of the city. Fortunately,
they'd all had the same prefix on their telephone
numbers. Keith had been unwittingly kind enough
to confirm the exact one. All that was left now

was to call her travel agent and make sure she
had a reservation when she arrived just before
midnight.

Dana didn't waste any time after that. She re-
packed her bag, throwing dirty clothes into the
hamper and stuffing in some new separates and
one good dress in case Marc would get around
to speaking to her and possibly take her out to
dinner. Since she'd made the hotel reservation
under her own name, there was no reason to
think that he'd be tipped off before she arrived.

Not that he'd expect her to keep on answering
to Mrs. Elliott. Dana paused for a minute in the
process of stuffing two new packages of nylons
in the top pocket of her case. Even a Puritan
Father couldn't have objected to their behavior
while she'd played at being Marc's wife. Other
than a few comments and that final farewell,
Marc hadn't shown the slightest interest in having the "game as well as the name." Which was
the way she wanted it, of course.

The trouble was—nobody would believe her.
Even Keith would raise his eyebrows and re-
quire some convincing. Which was why Marc
had abandoned the play-acting *and her* in Lexington, she told herself. Not that he wanted to see
the back of her as quickly as possible. And if she
believed that, she might as well go along with a
bridge for sale in Brooklyn.

She took a minute longer to debate the advis-
ability of her following Marc to San Juan. Chances
were, if she found him, he'd take about ten seconds to tell her to vamoose. Definitely he

wouldn't welcome her with open arms; the best she could hope for was a peaceful co-existence in the same hotel with a few shared dinners or lunches.

At least he owed her that, she told herself as she resumed her packing. She had a week of her vacation left, and spending it in Puerto Rico sounded a lot better than crawling the malls in Dallas during the summer heat wave.

Checking her watch, she realized that her shuttle bus connection to the airport was due in five minutes. She spent that closing her suitcase and putting it next to the door before setting the apartment thermostat for the time she'd be away. She thought about penning a note to Keith and then decided against it, choosing instead to call him once she arrived at her hotel.

After that, it was back to basics as she reached the airport and found that her direct flight to the Puerto Rican capital was only a half hour late. Even the long wait for takeoff didn't particularly bother her since she was following her instincts instead of logic.

She wasn't quite so cheerful when they landed at the San Juan airport four and a half hours later. Looking out at the darkness as they taxied toward the terminal, Dana suddenly became aware that her breakfast in Lexington seemed a long time ago and while the spirit was still very willing, her flesh was in need of a soft mattress without any turbulence.

The terminal was unbelievably crowded even at that hour, and when she finally got her bag,

she found the queue for taxis both long and
noisy.

There were more than the usual quota of vans
and limousines from the popular hotels and re-
sorts, Dana noted. Unfortunately, there was
nothing that bore the sign of Reforma-San Juan.

It was probably ten minutes before she was
able to get up close enough to the head of the
line that she could join the shouting matches between the drivers and other determined passen-
gers. Since she was going to the old sector of
town, she was turned down by two cabbies before a middle-aged driver took pity on her and
told her to get in.

As they pulled out of the crowded terminal,
he informed her that it was the last trip of his
shift and her hotel was on the way. So much for
her conviction that her woeful expression had
had any effect on him, Dana thought with inner
amusement. Now, all she could hope was that
the decrepit automobile would make it as far as
the old section of the city.

Unfortunately, they were only partway there
and passing through a rather unsavory section of
town, when a sudden lurch showed that one of
the tires wasn't cooperating.

The driver let loose a violent comment which
didn't bear translation, but kept driving on the
busy highway. Seeing Dana's puzzled expression
as they continued to lurch along, he said, "This
place is not safe to stop."

"But you'll ruin your tire . . ."

He shrugged. "There's nothing to ruin. We can

pull in at a gas station down a few blocks. I just hope the spare is a little better."

Dana nodded sympathetically and wondered what she was supposed to do while the change was taking place. A glance outside confirmed his opinion of the neighborhood, and there weren't any empty taxis cruising the busy highway.

When they pulled into the small gas station a few minutes later, she was glad to see a mini-market close by which was brightly lighted and full of customers. Before the driver could get out she gestured toward it. "Is it all right if I go over there and find something to drink while you're changing the tire?"

"*Sí, sí.*" Then, switching to English, "You stay near."

"Very near," she assured him. And after getting out of the car, she lingered a moment to look at the remnants of the tire. "I wish you luck."

"I need it, *señora.*"

His casual use of the term made Dana nod but give him a puzzled glance before she started walking toward the food store. Then it all became clear as she saw that she was still wearing the plain gold band Marc had given her in Kentucky. She started to take it off but paused again, reluctant for some reason to remove it. It might be better to keep it on since she was traveling alone, she told herself and wished she could believe her reasoning.

After purchasing two cans of soda and some cookies at the store, she walked back to the service station. She was happy to see that the spare

was apparently okay and now in place. The
driver accepted her gift of the cold soda with
profuse thanks and waved her back into the cab
with a courtly gesture.

The stop, however, made her arrival at the
hotel even later than she'd planned. When she
was finally deposited on the worn stone steps it
was close to midnight. The cab driver gallantly
took her luggage into the small foyer and deposited it in front of the reservations desk where an
unsmiling clerk awaited her.

From his appraisal, Dana could only surmise
that he didn't like the economic troubles between Puerto Rico and the United States or that
she had interrupted his coffee break.

"You wanted something, *señora*?"

She was too tired to respond as she was
tempted—like "What in the dickens do you
think I'm standing here for?" Instead, she said
in a carefully level voice, "I'm Dana McIntyre.
I believe I have a reservation. A confirmed reservation," she added warningly, just in case he
was tempted to say that they'd given her room
away hours ago.

"I will see, *señora*," was as far as his welcome
went, and he disappeared into a tiny alcove next
to the counter, ostensibly to check his records.

Dana's gaze immediately focused on the old-
fashioned ledger open on the counter in front of
her. Evidently in Old San Juan some establish-
ments didn't believe in everything's being done
by computer. She took another quick look toward

the alcove and then flipped back the register to
the previous page.

Marc's name was at the very bottom. M. Elliott, was all it said except for the wonderful
number 302 penciled in after it.

Dana turned the page back as if it were scald-
ing hot and when the clerk reappeared a few
seconds later, she was leaning on the counter ostensibly fascinated by a tray of brochures extol-
ling San Juan amenities.

"I found your reservation," the man admitted
almost reluctantly. "You are very late."

"So was the airplane," she told him, and
reached for a pen. "Shall I sign something?"

He indicated the register and watched her put
her name down before producing a key. "You
have room 204. Unfortunately, it is over the
street, but there is not much traffic at this time
of night."

Which left about twelve hours on the clock
when she wouldn't be so fortunate, Dana decided. After a quick look at his smug expression,
she knew it wouldn't do her any good to argue.
Not with the night clerk, anyway. Perhaps in the
morning, she'd meet a more sympathetic soul.
"It really doesn't matter," she told him, and had
the pleasure of seeing disappointment cloud his
expression.

He still had one more trump card. "Unfortunately, at this time of night, there is no one to
help you with your luggage."

"Think nothing of it." She kept her voice light.
"Possibly there is an elevator ..."

He had to own up to that. He gestured to it just beyond the foyer as he handed her a room key.

Dana took it and abandoned any more conversation, happy to just get to her room. After that, she'd go up to Marc's room and see if he were receiving. That would be better than trying to phone, she decided, since another feature of the hotel front desk had been an old-fashioned switchboard. She had no doubt that her chum on the counter would either let her phone go unanswered or listen to every word of the conversation if he did connect her with Marc.

The elevator wheezed a bit before arriving at her floor. Which fitted her status exactly, Dana decided. She was wheezing herself before she managed to get her luggage down the long tiled corridor to room 204.

Once inside, she saw the usual twin beds with pale yellow ruffled spreads that looked as if they might have come from a 1930s movie. There was a combination desk and dressing table with a chair in front of it. The chair had wrought iron arms and legs so that no one would be tempted to linger too long. Over by the French doors, which apparently opened over the street, was another chair—this time in striped yellow and white—which looked more comfortable. It faced a twelve-inch television set with an out-of-date program guide atop it.

Dana pulled open the French door to gaze out onto a tiny wrought iron balcony, but as soon as she felt the humid air, she quickly closed it again. Wandering around the end of the beds, she found a white-tiled bathroom which looked old but was still serviceable. She lingered back by one of the beds to pull down the spread and test the pillow. It was so sturdy that it could have been there since the Spanish generals arrived in the 1500s.

Sorrowfully shaking her head, she decided that everything looked bad because it was late and she was tired. There was also the possibility that Marc might very well close the door in her face after telling her to go home.

If that was in the cards, she decided she might as well look as good as possible, and took another five minutes to comb her hair and renew her makeup. She realized that she was simply putting off the moment of truth since midnight wasn't the preferred time to go calling on anybody.

She brushed her hair back from her face and made sure that her room key was safely tucked in her shoulder purse before letting herself out into the empty tiled hallway.

The stairway door was a lot closer than the rickety elevator so she opened it carefully and was glad to see that it was at least dimly lighted. The sound of hurrying footsteps down below showed that she wasn't the only person choosing that exit rather than the elevator.

She trudged up the metal steps, turning wearily at the landing before taking the final set. When she reached the third floor, she pulled open the nearby door with some difficulty and then frowned as a blast of music came down the

hallway. Somewhere nearby, someone was tossing a whale of a party.

That wouldn't improve Marc's disposition, she
thought. Unless he'd been invited, too.

She peered at the numbers on the rooms, wishing that the hotel had thought to install a few
more electric lights. Marc's room was close to
the source of hilarity and she was smiling as she
paused in front of his door to knock.

The first touch of her knuckles pushed the
door slightly open and her smile faded abruptly.
It was dark in the hallway of the room and there
was no answer to her whispered, "Marc? Are
you there?"

She gingerly pushed the door again, trying to
get past whatever obstacle was holding it ajar.
Then she heard a low moan and her voice rose
in panic. "Marc! Is that you?"

"Who the hell are you?" came a muttered
curse from beyond the door.

"It's me," she said ungrammatically. "I mean
I—Dana." The last came out almost desperately.

"I'm losing my mind," he groaned.

"If you'd move away from the door, I could
prove that you're not," she said, shoving frantically against the wood.

That time it gave way, and Dana almost fell
over Marc as he tried to stand erect. "Oh, God!
My head!" Marc groaned as soon as they re-
gained their balance. Then, taking another look
at her in the dim light from the hall he said, "It
is you. I thought I was out of my head." And

putting his hand up to it, he added, "Right now, I wish to hell that I was."

"What's happened? Did you fall?"

"Only after somebody hit me with some brass knuckles. At least that's what it felt like."

"But where? Who?"

"Down by the square," he said after a moment's pause. "Luckily whoever it was got interrupted by some passersby before he could do too much damage. I was able to duck into an all-night grocery and call a cab to come back here. Unfortunately, I ran out of steam after I got the door unlocked."

"But whoever it was could have followed you," Dana said, staying close as he flopped down in the chair by the window.

"What a little ray of sunshine you are," he said, grimacing at the blood on his fingers when he explored the side of his forehead. "And what in the devil are you doing in Puerto Rico? You're supposed to be in Dallas."

Dana's ego rose a trifle. Marc hadn't reacted as if he hated her. Instead, he sounded like a man who'd had his plans go awry—possibly plans that involved keeping her safe. She took a deep breath and decided that there wasn't time to debate the subject just then. "Look, it isn't safe for you here. It makes a lot more sense for you to come down to my room. I've registered under my own name so they won't connect the two of us."

"Don't go so fast," he said irritably. "You mean that you're staying here at the hotel?"

"Down on the second floor." She headed toward the bathroom and came back with his toiletries case. "I can't manage to carry your suitcase and hang on to you. This time, you'll have to travel light." Detouring to his open suitcase, she asked, "Where are your pajamas?"

"You'll have to settle for that travel robe," he said, obviously in pain.

"Okay. I'll put it in this attaché case."

"For Pete's sake, don't lose the papers in there."

"I didn't lose a thing," she said, zipping it up. "Come on, let's get out of here."

"I guess you're right. At least until I can swallow enough aspirin to keep the top of my head from coming off," he replied wearily. "Am I hearing things, or is that really rock music?"

"There's a party next door. If you didn't have a headache already, you would get one after staying in this room another ten minutes. Come on, lean on me. If we meet anybody, they'll just think you've had too much to drink at the party."

"Great." Obviously, he wasn't enchanted by that idea but was in no shape to object.

They got out into the corridor without encountering anyone. Marc watched her pull his door tightly closed to lock it and then stayed by her side as they headed for the elevator. Dana kept her free arm around his waist and, after seeing him in the brighter light by the elevator, she said, "If there's anybody around on my hall, duck your head. You look as if you'd lost a championship fight."

"I believe you. Otherwise I wouldn't be going along with this lousy idea of yours. I don't know why in the hell you had to get yourself involved in this. The whole idea of sending you home was to avoid it."

"I finally figured that out," she told him with some satisfaction as the empty elevator finally arrived. "C'mon. You can read me the riot act later."

Marc winced as the elevator jerked its way down a floor and the doors opened with a metallic rasp.

"Company," Dana warned in a whisper as they stepped out and discovered a couple halfway down the corridor.

"Oh, damn!" Marc muttered, and ducked his head as if he were nuzzling her neck and shoulder.

The older couple passed them, managing a couple of disapproving looks in the process.

"They're probably discussing my hourly rate," she told Marc as she heard a room door slam behind them.

"God knows what they're saying about me," he murmured. "How much farther?"

"Right here," she announced, pulling to a stop in front of her door and searching through her purse for the key. "Open sesame." Urging Marc ahead of her, she said, "Pick either bed."

It didn't take any more urging for him to almost collapse on the nearest mattress.

Dana carefully put a double lock on the door and then moved inside quietly to survey him. "So far, so good."

As hushed as her voice had been, Marc evidently heard every word. "Don't get too excited about it," he warned flatly. "Where in the devil do we go from here?"

Chapter Seven

Dana tried to make her tone casual. "I'd say the first thing on the list is to clean you up. After that, we'll see about getting a nice close-mouthed doctor."

"Over my dead body!"

"In that case, there'd be no use calling in a doctor," she told him, heading for the bathroom to get a wet face cloth. Her first step on the tiled floor almost sent her sprawling.

The startled shriek she let out brought Marc upright, clutching his head with a groan. "What's wrong?" he managed to get out.

"I'm sorry." She sent an apologetic glance at him over her shoulder. "Something must be wrong with the air conditioner in here or something. The place is almost awash with . . ."

"Condensation?"

"'That's the nice way of putting it. Anyhow, if you come in here, hang onto something solid. This floor feels as if it's been greased." She realized that she was babbling but it seemed like a good thing to lighten the mood of the moment. Finally emerging with a damp face cloth and a fresh towel, she settled gingerly on the edge of Marc's bed. "Can you do this or—"

"I can manage," he cut in brusquely, and struggled to get upright against the pillow.

"Let me help you," she said, surrendering the face cloth and reaching behind him to punch up the pillow. "I'll get the other pillow from my bed," she added, going around the end of his. "We might as well use them for propping you up. If the Japanese ever give up their porcelain ones, these would be the natural successor. Not only do you wake up with a headache, you get a stiff neck thrown in."

A reluctant grin softened his expression for an instant. "You don't like my choice of hotels. Believe me, I did have a reason," he added. "It seemed good at the time." Dabbing gingerly at the abrasion on his head with the wet face cloth, he went on, "Of course, there's every chance that I just ran into the ordinary garden variety of mugger."

"But you don't think so, do you?"

He shook his head carefully, but winced even then. "Not really. How's your medicine chest?"

"What do you mean?" she asked, frowning.

"Look, stop sounding like you need to call the Doctors Mayo. A couple of aspirin should do the trick." He held out the bloody face cloth with a disgusted grimace. "And maybe a couple of Band-Aids."

Dana took the face cloth and tossed it into the bathroom sink for rinsing out later. "Are you sure? And don't try that stiff-upper-lip stuff. If you think you might have a concussion—"

"I don't," he cut in ruthlessly. "I wish to God that you'd stop fussing." Then, glancing upward to see her carefully blank expression, he added, "Oh, hell—I'm sorry. That's as good an apology as you're going to get from me tonight. If it weren't for the fact that I'm imposing on your hospitality, I'd like to wring your neck."

"Right now, you haven't enough strength," she informed him, feeling better. "I'll hunt up the medicine while you dry off."

"I don't want to get blood on your towel," he protested. "Knowing this place, it won't do any good to call down to the housekeeping department and request any extra ones."

"You're probably right." After rummaging in the top of her suitcase, she came back to his bedside with a small zipper bag. Taking out two adhesive bandages, she surveyed his forehead carefully. "It looks to me as if it's clotting nicely. Two of these things should do it—unless you sleep on your stomach and rub them off on the pillowcase."

"You have to be kidding," he told her in a wry tone, and started to get up.

"Where do you think you're going?"

He paused with one foot on the carpet. "I need a mirror to stick them on."

She pushed him back on the pillows, thankful that he didn't put up much resistance. From the feel of his muscles, she knew that normally she couldn't try such a high-handed maneuver. "I'll put them on." Then, seeing his frown, she said, "Be sensible. You don't want to start the bleeding again by larking around." Before he could protest, she tore open the bandages and as gently as possible pressed them over the nasty abrasion. Straightening, she dropped the wrappings in the wastebasket and then shook two aspirins from a plastic container into his hand. "Just a second and I'll get you some water."

When she went into the bathroom and ran water from the cold water tap the silence from the bedroom seemed almost as chilling as the blast of cold air that came from the ceiling vent. No, not quite, she decided, as several drops of icy water soaked her shoulders. Without waiting any longer, she filled the glass and went back into the bedroom.

Marc took it from her and swallowed the aspirin without comment. As he handed the glass back, he said, "You look ready to commit murder. What is it now?"

"It's just that when I take a shower, I prefer to be undressed and in the tub," she said shrugging uncomfortably. "That bathroom's impossible. What happens if I turn off the air conditioning?"

"I'd hate to try it without some fresh air in the room." His gaze went to the French doors which opened out onto the tiny balcony.

"That sounds like a good answer," she said, walking over to them. "On the second floor, we certainly don't have to worry about anyone climbing up from the street."

"Not unless they're training to be James Bond."

"Exactly." She managed to pull the doors open with a slight effort. "Umm. It's a little humid outside, but that's all right. After living in Texas, that's nothing new." Walking back to where she'd dropped his attaché case, she said, "Now, you just need to get into your robe and then have a good night's sleep."

A pained look came over Marc's face. "Do you have to sound like a Cub Scout leader? I admit that my head's bruised, but my brains aren't scrambled so don't sound so damned chirpy."

Dana couldn't admit that she was rattling on to cover up her nervousness. There certainly wasn't anything wrong with sharing her room with a man, especially one who looked as if the only exertion he could manage right then was struggling into his robe. On the other hand, it wouldn't hurt him to act a little more like the Good Humor Man rather than trying for the role of Ivan the Terrible.

Some of her thoughts must have shown because Marc pushed himself up on the bed and swung his feet over the side. "I wouldn't exactly blame you if you tossed me over the balcony. How long does it take that aspirin to work?"

"I should think any time now." She handed him the robe. "Shall I go into the bathroom while you change?"

A crooked smile appeared on his face for just an instant. "So very, very discreet and ladylike. Being a modern woman, I thought that you'd offer to help me undress."

Dana could feel her cheeks getting warm, but

she didn't let on. "I can manage that if you'd prefer."

"Forget it." There wasn't any humor in his voice as he started toward the bathroom.

"For heaven's sake—watch out for that slippery floor."

"Yes, mother." There was a definite snarl that time as he closed the bathroom door behind him.

Men! Dana thought irritably. What she should have done was simply gone over and started taking off his pants. Dollars to doughnuts, he would have set a new record heading for some privacy then!

As she heard the sound of water running in the bathroom basin, she went over to put her bag on a luggage rack and unzip it. This would be a good time to get out her own night things and be ready for a second shift in the bathroom. She was too tired to take a shower, and besides she felt that the drippy air conditioner had already managed to get her damp in parts. The humidity was doing the rest. When she got up in the morning, she'd be better able to cope.

For an instant, she wondered if she'd done the right thing in not calling a doctor for Marc. There certainly didn't seem to be anything wrong with his responses and he looked as wide awake as ever. She could check on him during the night and make sure that his sleep seemed to be normal.

The bathroom door opened at that point and Marc emerged in his robe, carrying his clothes over one arm.

"I'll take those for you and hang them up," Dana said, moving over quickly.

"Thanks. Since my wardrobe's a little limited, I'd better not toss them in a corner. Incidentally," he said, sinking onto the bed, "you're right about that condensation. It felt like the inside of an oyster in there." Pushing back the covers and shoving his feet between the sheets, he added, "It's not only the bathroom. If I didn't know better, I'd think they made up this bed with a wet wash. And don't say anything about my choice of hotels."

Dana's shoulders were shaking with laughter. "I wasn't going to. Actually, I was too busy listening to something else."

A frown creased his forehead. "What do you mean? There isn't any traffic, is there?"

She shook her head and put up a hand to silence him. "Just listen. It's a very distinctive high-pitched whine."

After an instant's silence, Marc groaned. "My God! Mosquitoes!"

"I'm afraid so. We either drown in condensation or get eaten alive unless we want to spend the rest of the night under the sheets. The wet sheets," she added before he could correct her.

"We might as well get drunk. It appears that a hangover is the only thing we're missing," he said in disgust.

"Welcome to San Juan." Dana couldn't hide the weariness in her voice. "How do you vote? Cold air or fresh air?"

"I'd rather take my chances on staying afloat.

And don't suggest trying to turn off the air conditioning. I'm not that much of a hero."

"That makes two of us." She was struggling to get the balcony doors closed again and finally made it. "How's your headache?"

"It must be getting better," he admitted, touching the bandages with careful fingers. "That mosquito attack made me forget it completely for the moment."

"I'm glad of that." She collected her pajamas and robe from the top of her suitcase and started for the bathroom. "It doesn't sound like you have a concussion, after all."

"I shouldn't have to convince you, of all people, how hard-headed I am," he said ruefully.

"That's true." She kept her voice carefully level so that he wouldn't know how his half-naked lounging figure was doing catastrophic things to her pulse rate. "Well, if you don't need any special nursing at the moment, I'll get changed, too."

Once in the bathroom with the door firmly closed behind her, she took an instant to lean against it, wondering how she was going to be in such close contact with Marc without laying her emotions down on the ground in front of him so that they could be trampled.

Not that he'd do it deliberately. He'd be the soul of courtesy to Keith's sister. After all, it wouldn't do to make waves with a business partner. Unless, of course, she started to cling and bare her innermost, embarrassing yearnings. Then he'd sever their relationship fast and finally.

Leaning over to change her shoes for slippers, she came back to reality in a hurry as the moisture on the cold tiled floor immediately penetrated her nylons. "Damn!" she muttered in exasperation. "Damn! Damn! Damn!"

"What's the matter?"

Marc's worried voice penetrated the same way as the cold water. "Nothing," she called back, and then remembered the time of night. Opening the door a bit, she stuck her head around it. "Sorry. I just uh—uh slipped a bit. I won't be long."

After that, she changed rapidly, doing her best to avoid the icy water dripping from above. The water from the tap was lukewarm and she splashed it over her face. Then she reached automatically for her toothbrush and remembered that it was still in her cosmetic bag on her suitcase. "Damn!" she said again, but in a low voice, and used the corner of her towel as a substitute.

Examining her pale reflection in the mirror when she'd finished, she realized that she was simply stalling for time, unsure of how to act once she left the bathroom.

As it happened, she needn't have worried. When she finally turned off the light and brushed the last drops of "condensation" from her shoulders before going back into the bedroom, she found that Marc had turned off the overhead light. That left only the dim lamp on the table between their beds still on.

She cast a quick glance at his motionless figure and found that he was propped up against the headboard watching her through half-closed lids. Even though he was ostensibly half-asleep, she knew that he hadn't missed an inch of her short aqua pajamas or their matching robe.

"I was beginning to wonder if I should send in a search team," he said finally.

"Sorry—I didn't mean to keep you up." She made a production out of dropping her clothes into the open suitcase. "Can I get you anything before I turn out the light?"

"Not unless you have access to a T-bone steak or some mosquito repellent." He sat up straighter and pulled the extra pillow from behind his back, tossing it over to her bed. "You'll need that."

"Not as much as you do," she responded.

"For Lord's sake—don't argue," he said wearily. "I'll be fine. Just turn out the light, will you?"

"Yes, of course," she said apologetically as she turned back the cover on her bed. "Don't be stupid about waking me up if there's anything I can do in what's left of the night."

"You mean that you make house calls?"

Dana was determined that his wry probing wasn't going to damage her hard-won dignity. "As far as aspirins and Band-Aids go, I'm unbeatable." She drew in her breath sharply as she put her feet down into the damp sheets.

"Clammy, isn't it?" Marc commented.

"I'm sure that it will be fine as soon as I get used to it," she lied as she reached over to turn off the lamp on the night table. "Good night," she said then, trying to sound brisk.

A creaking spring was evidence that Marc was trying to get comfortable. "I wish I could find something good about it."

After that, there wasn't any more attempt at conversation. Dana pulled her feet up from the bottom of the bed, hoping that the fetal position might be warmer. She tried to ignore the pale pink light that seeped through the curtains on the balcony doors; evidently there was a neon sign that had gone unnoticed earlier. There was no chance of ignoring the high-pitched whine of several mosquitoes who were still cruising the room looking for a suitable landing place. One seemed to have her as his number-one target and was circling lower and lower over her ear until she couldn't stand it any longer and jerked the damp sheet over her head.

She managed that mummy-like position for about five minutes while she debated the merits of suffocation over being eaten alive, and finally decided to try a compromise. That involved finding a small breathing hole in the sheet wrapped around her head. It worked fairly well—apparently well enough that her eyes closed and she fell into a restless sleep.

It was about two hours later that a strange noise brought her upright. "What's going on?" she said groggily, trying to peer through the pink gloom of the room.

"Nothing." Marc emerged from the bathroom to sink down on the edge of his bed again. "I didn't mean to wake you, but I knocked a glass into the basin before I found the light in there." As he saw her start to get out of bed, he put up a detaining palm. "Relax, it didn't break."

"Ummm." She remained poised on the edge of her bed, still half-asleep.

"I was looking for some more aspirin," he went on. "If you'll just tell me where you hid it . . ."

"Get back in bed," she told him, fully awake by then. Rubbing the goose bumps on her arms, she decided that she'd never leave home again without a pair of long-sleeved pajamas. "I'll get it for you."

As he pulled the covers up, she found her slippers and then unearthed the aspirin tablets. Making sure that she didn't drop the bathroom glass, she ran water in it and went back to Marc's bedside. "I hope it isn't too soon for you to be taking more pills."

"It's fine," he said, gulping them down.

"How *is* your head?" she asked, "Or is that a silly question."

"It's settled down to a dull roar, but I've had worse hangovers in my salad days." As he handed back the glass, he came into contact with her fingers. "Lord, you feel frozen."

"If you think they're bad, you should feel my feet," she said, trying to sound amused by the whole thing. "On second thought, you'd better not. If I'd known what the nights were like here, I'd have brought a fur coat."

He was surveying her closely in the dim lamp

light. "Good Lord! Even your teeth are chattering."

"I thought I was hearing castanets," she replied, determined to avoid the doom and gloom. "If you don't want any more water, I'll dump it out."

He waited until she was back from the bathroom before he said, "You'll never get to sleep again if you don't get warm."

She made a helpless gesture. "I don't know what I can do about it. The only coat I brought is a nylon topper in case of rain and there aren't any extra blankets in the closet. There isn't room for a gerbil in that closet—let alone bed linen."

"I know." He sounded weary as he shifted over in his bed. "Well, that only leaves one alternative. We'll combine forces. Pull your spread over on top of mine and bring your pillow. I'm only chivalrous up to a point." When she opened her mouth to complain, he said, "And don't argue. Even Keith would sanction this arrangement rather than have you in the hospital with double pneumonia."

"I thought pneumonia was caused by a virus."

He eyed her immobile fingers severely. "If you don't hurry up, I'll rescind my offer. And you don't have to worry about maidenly modesty. I'd have trouble making time with a *Playboy* centerfold tonight, so if I lay a finger on you, it'll be strictly as a substitute heating pad."

Which put her right in the same category as a long-toothed maiden aunt, Dana thought. He was undoubtedly making his proclamation to erase any reservations she might have about sharing his bed. On the other hand, he didn't have to sound so damned smug and self-righteous about it.

"Your time's running out," he said, rubbing the back of his neck wearily.

"Oh, all right." She went over to her bed and tugged the thin spread loose, putting it atop his. Then she tossed her pillow alongside his with more force than necessary, only regretting her movement when she saw Marc wince. She debated apologizing and then decided against it.

"Do you usually go off into a brown study in the middle of the night?" He had pulled back the sheet on her side, and apparently was keeping a grip on his temper with difficulty.

There was nothing she could say to that without leading to more trouble, and by then she was too tired to throw down any more gauntlets. Sitting on the edge of the mattress, she took off her slippers and then debated sleeping in her nylon robe. It would be a nuisance if she tried to turn over, so she shrugged it off.

"Very wise," Marc said laconically. "Now, turn off the light, will you?"

She did that without comment and stretched out carefully on her edge of the mattress, doing her best to avoid touching his masculine figure.

There were several moments of silence and then Marc let out an exasperated sigh before his arm snaked out and pulled her tight against him. "The object of the lesson was to get you warm," he said in the vicinity of her ear as he maneu-

vered her spoon-fashion against his long body.
"And stop squirming, for God's sake."

"I'm not squirming!"

"Well, whatever you call it. If you want to
keep everything on a nice platonic level, just
breathe. Get it?"

Dana took a deep breath and finally muttered,
"Got it. I wasn't trying anything."

"I know that," he growled. "Sometimes I don't
think you have any more sense than John. And
don't try flouncing away," he added, his arm like
a steel bar at her waist. "The object of this exercise is to exchange body heat in a gentlemanly
way. If you keep on breaking the rules, I'll toss
you back to your bed or—"

"Or what?" she asked daringly.

"Let's just say that by morning you'll be on
the first plane back to Texas a sadder and wiser
woman."

Which didn't tell her anything, Dana concluded, and decided to quit while she was a little
bit ahead. She made herself relax, trying to pretend that the strong masculine body behind her
was simply an anonymous source of heat.

Marc gave a muffled sound of satisfaction and
loosened his grip on her waist. "That's better.
Now maybe we can get some sleep for what's
left of the night."

Dana couldn't think of anything to respond to
that so she closed her eyes and decided to be
grateful for the newfound comfort that was
slowly penetrating the bed.

She must have slept after that because it was

Marc's moaning that brought her awake the next time. Struggling to sit up, she squinted to see her watch dial and found that it was just before dawn. Marc turned restlessly onto his back then and muttered something under his breath. Clearly, he was still reliving the painful events of the evening.

Dana wondered if she should get up and find another dose of aspirin to help him rest or whether she should go back to her own bed so that he could be more comfortable. She'd almost decided on the latter plan when he turned onto his stomach, putting his arm possessively across her breast and letting his head rest against her shoulder.

As Dana carefully lifted her arm to get more comfortable, he moved even closer and seemed to drift into a deeper sleep. Either the nightmare was over or he was used to finding a feminine form beside him.

That thought made Dana stiffen defensively. In turn, Marc's clasp tightened at her breast. She drew in her breath sharply but his even breathing didn't vary. Obviously he was sound asleep.

She debated her options then and found that it was difficult to keep things platonic when the man who occupied all her thoughts awake or sleeping had her in a possessive sensual hold.

In fact, he was doing just what she'd hoped for about two hours after he'd met her in North Carolina. Only it hadn't occurred to her that it would happen when he was sound asleep!

She let out a rueful sigh and nudged her head

a little closer to his pillow. What was it the British said—'Relax and think of England.' At that particular moment, she could do a lot better than that! She took another look in the half-light and observed Marc's drawn and pale features. If ever a man needed his sleep, he was the one.

Pity, she thought to herself as she snuggled against him. Now she'd never know whether all the trailing fingers and heavy breathing in romance novels really worked.

The next time she stirred and cautiously opened her eyes, it was to find that sunshine was penetrating the worn curtains on the balcony doors, replacing the pink neon of the night with brilliant light.

She also discovered that one side of her was toasty warm while the other was thirty degrees cooler. Opening her eyes still wider, she discerned that the warmth came from her proximity to Marc's long body and the cold section was practically without covering of any kind. After sitting up abruptly to pull her shortie pajamas further over her thighs, she turned to stare at the man next to her.

He was surveying her with bland interest, apparently not particularly concerned with the expanse of skin to which he'd been treated. "Good morning," he said finally.

"Uh—good morning," she managed, wondering how in the world her pajamas had gotten so twisted. "How do you feel this morning?"

"What category are you talking about?"

She shot him a suspicious look. "What do you mean?"

"I just wondered whether you were in the role of resident nurse or the woman currently sharing my bed." Seeing her brows draw together, he hastily changed his wording. "Sorry. Scratch the 'currently.'"

"Why bother?" She tried to sound suitably flippant, which wasn't easy two minutes after emerging from a sound sleep.

"You mean that you're comfortable in that latter category?"

She considered the options and then decided that she'd better follow reason rather than instinct. Swinging her feet to the floor, she said, "It sounds as if we play in different leagues."

"Maybe not." He was watching her closely.

She cast a reproving glance at the bandage on his head. "We'll never know. Since you're still in the category of 'walking wounded,' I'd better act as resident nurse."

All humor disappeared from his face and he favored her with his usual laconic expression. "You're right," he said tightening his robe. "Do you want to take first shift in the bathroom while I get dressed in here? After that, I'll leave you in peace and go back to my room."

"You can't do that," she said, pulling up on the threshold of the bathroom.

"Why not?"

"Because whoever cracked you on the head last night might be lurking in the hall this morning."

"Don't be ridiculous!"

"I'm *not* being ridiculous. What makes you think that he'll give up after one try?"

"Let's say that the odds are in my favor today."

Dana let out an exasperated sigh. "Do you suppose that you might explain a few things? Just enough to keep the 'little woman' happy."

His expression changed to the familiar frown. "What's eating you now? You can't complain about any harassment in sharing my bed."

"That never entered my mind." Even as she spoke, she knew that she sounded too defensive.

"The hell it didn't! You're madder than hops about it. Almost as mad as you'd be if I'd tried anything."

She raised her chin defiantly. "I certainly didn't have to worry last night. You had trouble even swallowing aspirin."

He pursed his lips as he thought about it. "You're probably right. On the other hand, I'm better this morning and I'd hate for you to go away disappointed." As he spoke, he reached out and yanked her against him.

"You can't—" she began, and then was silenced very effectively when his lips came down to cover hers in a kiss that was possessive and thorough.

Dana was vaguely aware that his hands were roaming every curve and she had no doubt that the thin nylon of her pajamas revealed only too well her response to his expert touch.

The kiss seemed to go on and on until Marc

finally, reluctantly, pushed her away. By that time, Dana was clinging to his robe to keep from sinking down in an inglorious heap at his feet.

"What was all that in aid of?" she finally managed to ask.

"I just wanted you to know that I'm practically back to normal. Any more bed sharing and the rules will be changed."

Her eyebrows shot up. "I'm quaking in my boots already. In the meantime, I wish you'd tell me what the deuce is going on."

All the humor left his face. "I suppose you have a right to know after taking care of me last night, but I prefer my third degrees after breakfast. Why don't I meet you down in the coffee shop in a half hour? That'll give me a chance to shower and change."

"You think that's better than room service?" she asked.

"Definitely. The room service here is as erratic as the air conditioning. If we're in the restaurant, we have a fifty-fifty chance for hot coffee." When he saw her worried expression, he gave her a gentle shove toward the bathroom. "Stop worrying. The halls will be cluttered with maids and porters, so nobody is going to linger and act suspicious. Besides, I'll be on my guard from now on. It could have been just a mugger last night, you know."

"But you don't think so," she probed.

He rubbed his head wearily. "No. Not really. Anyhow, today should see the end of it. Now, go on in and have your shower, unless you want an exhibition of the body beautiful."

He was starting to untie the belt on his robe as he spoke.

Dana stared at him for an instant in disbelief, knowing that he was doing it deliberately to push her into a hasty exit. She lingered just long enough to see the robe start to open before she turned and walked quickly away.

Behind her, she heard a masculine chuckle, but she had to satisfy her annoyance by slamming the bathroom door behind her. All that did was let down an extra shower of cool water from the air conditioning duct on the ceiling.

"Damnation!" she said aloud before starting to see the amusing side of things. After all, since she was headed for the shower, a little extra dampness didn't matter. And if Marc tried a dare like that another time, she'd simply sit down on the edge of the mattress and enjoy the show. Having been brought up with an older brother, the sight of a masculine body wouldn't be any great surprise!

A lukewarm shower helped her mood considerably, as did donning a coral linen-look dress with cap sleeves and a boat neckline to co-exist with the heat and humidity. She pulled her hair back from her face with a mock tortoise bandeau, again in deference to the humidity. A pair of coral flats completed the outfit and she gave a nod of approval at her reflection in the steamy mirror.

Marc hadn't left any reminders of his occupation except a rumpled bed. Dana stood staring at it for a moment, wondering what the management would think about two beds being used when the room was rented to a single person. Then she grinned as she decided it wouldn't be the first time it had happened. Or the first time that only one bed was occupied when the room was rented to a couple. Her imagination carried her a little further along that train of thought until she shook her head impatiently and picked up her purse.

It seemed easier to take the stairs than wait for the elevator, and she was relieved to find that they were unoccupied until she reached the ground floor. The sound of china rattling made her turn to the left, away from the reception area, and find her way to an attractive coffee shop. Her first impression was that of a tremendous aviary with even some brightly colored birds sitting in the tropical foliage around the edge of the room to solidify the impression. A high curved ceiling added to the impression of cathedral-like dimensions. In the midst of such grandeur, a dozen or so wrought iron tables with glass tops looked as if they were miniature-sized. Up a few steps to the right was a long wooden bar which evidently was the center of activity later in the day. This morning, there was a coffee urn placed at one end plus a dozen or so cups by the spigot.

Three of the tables were occupied, but Marc wasn't in evidence. Since there wasn't any movement from the two waiters leaning against the bar in the midst of a heated discussion, Dana found a nearby table and pulled out a chair.

The noise of its scraping on the tile caused the waiters to look around and the nearest one to saunter toward her. He reached the table in time to help push her chair in and say, "*Buenos dias, señora. Como—*"

Dana cut in politely, "Good morning. Could I have a menu, please?"

"*Seguro.*" He caught himself and added, "Of course. You are alone?"

"No. There'll be a gentleman joining me."

"I see. Would you like coffee or juice while you're waiting?"

"Orange juice would be nice, thank you. I'll have coffee later with the rest of my breakfast."

"Very good." He glanced up to see Marc coming toward the table. "This is the gentleman?"

"That is the gentleman," she confirmed with gentle irony. Then to Marc, "Good morning. Would you like some juice now?"

"No, thanks." He pulled out a chair beside her. "I wouldn't turn down a cup of coffee though."

"*Inmediatemente, señor.*" The waiter's relaxed manner changed to all business and he scurried off.

Dana was surveying Marc with some amusement. "You look quite different from last night."

"There's nothing like a good night's sleep," he countered, not bothering to hide his own amusement. "Or don't you agree"

She refused to follow the bait. "Absolutely. If

you didn't have that bruise on your head, I'd never know that you'd been down for the count."

He put up careful fingers to touch it. "I thought it looked better than being plastered. What are you eating?"

His abrupt change of subject caught her off-guard. "I hadn't decided. Maybe just toast and coffee." The decision came as the waiter deposited a large orange juice in front of her and a cup of coffee in front of Marc. "Toast and coffee please," she added.

"And you, sir?"

"Two poached eggs and toast to go along with this," Marc said, gesturing toward his coffee.

Dana was observing him under lowered lashes, thinking how well-groomed he looked in a dark brown sport shirt with his khaki chino trousers. His tanned skin helped hide the lines around his eyes which showed that he hadn't completely recovered from his night's experience.

When the waiter departed with the menus, Marc's glance turned back to her and Dana quickly concentrated on her glass of juice. "You said that you'd tell me what's going on," she said briskly.

Marc's jaw seemed even sterner than usual as he searched for words. "The reason I'm here is to try and make sure that my good friend George doesn't get out of Puerto Rico heading south," he said finally.

"Like Brazil?" Dana stared at him until he nodded, and then she went on, "But how do you know he's even here?"

"I was pretty sure before and I'd bet money on it now, since the airport authorities have confirmed that Michelle arrived in the middle of the night."

Dana bit the edge of her bottom lip as she tried to concentrate. "I still don't understand. Why Puerto Rico? Why didn't he go straight on down and avoid any chance of extradition?"

"The reason he's here is that this is home base for him even though he's lived in the United States off and on for years. However, he's going to be slapped with an arrest warrant by U.S. authorities if he doesn't get out of the territory fast. I imagine he's closing operations and trying to line up some expensive lawyers."

"And you think he's been behind all this trouble you've had?"

"I don't think—I know."

Dana shuddered involuntarily, hearing the ominous tone in Marc's voice. "Okay—I'll take your word for it. But why all the fuss because a company is losing money? That doesn't call for hitting people over the head or running them off the road." She shot him a perplexed glance. "Or does it?"

"Not that alone, maybe, but when you drag the Federal Government into it—Uncle Sam starts flexing his muscles." Noting her still puzzled face, Marc sighed and took another sip of coffee. "George carefully leaked some 'official' memos also marked 'top secret' which announced that the mammoth industrial park the corporation was building was going to be in the middle of a nuclear waste dump."

"Oh, boy!"

"Exactly." Marc's expression was just as grim as his tone. "Sales agreements and leases for the property were canceled so fast that the legal department couldn't keep up. It wasn't until the prices and the profits went down that some unknown buyers came out of nowhere."

"To catch an investment on the way up."

"Exactly. But then the big thing was to prove it. Namely, to find a copy of the 'memo' and prove that George was behind it." Marc paused long enough to let the waiter deposit their breakfasts in front of them and pour more coffee. When he'd gone back to rejoin the other waiters lounging by the bar, Marc went on, "We were finally able to do it during this last trip to Lexington. George must have been tipped off."

"Was that why we were run off the road?" she asked, interrupting.

"At that point, I suspect he was just trying to throw a wrench in the works. George is too smooth to be concerned with any real mayhem that could be traced back to him."

"Of course, if you'd broken your neck by driving into the ditch . . ." She let her voice trail off suggestively.

"He would have sent a magnificent wreath to the funeral," Marc said, putting preserves on his piece of toast. "Sure you don't want an egg or something?"

Dana shook her head decisively. "I'm not a morning person."

"Oh, I don't know. I thought you looked extremely attractive curled up against my shoulder. Innocent and sort of *jeune fille*, if you know what I mean. Quite different from what you choose to present when you're awake."

Dana was so surprised by the turn of his conversation that she could only stare at him for an instant. "I'm not sure I like that *jeune fille* role," she said finally.

"It was meant as a compliment. You're just supposed to say 'thank you' and pass the rest of the preserves."

"Thank you," she managed, shoving the dish toward him. "May I say that you now sound definitely back to normal."

"What makes me suspect that isn't meant as a compliment." He heaped preserves on a final bite of toast, showing that her verbal assault hadn't affected his appetite, and then finished the last of his eggs as a final gesture. "Anyhow, today is the moment of truth. We'd damned well better find him or he'll get away with all those millions he's been collecting."

Dana nodded, her thoughts still back on his comment about his observations of her while sharing his bed. She'd never had anyone say such a thing before—probably because she'd never been curled up against a masculine shoulder at dawn. It would have been nice if he'd said a little bit more.

"So that's why I want you to stay out of the

way. Are you even listening to what I'm telling you?"

Marc's aggrieved tone managed to penetrate finally and Dana took refuge in rearranging her toast crust on the plate. "Certainly I'm listening. I'm—I'm—"

"I can tell that you didn't miss a syllable," he said with more than usual exasperation. "Dammit—pay attention. I don't want to find you slumped in a corner someplace."

"I'll be careful," she began, only to have him cut her off.

"Besides, if George or Michelle see you, they'll be sure that we're onto their game."

Dana did look up then to meet his accusing gaze. "What makes me think that you're worried less about my neck than the success of your whatchamacallit."

"That whatchamacallit runs into eight figures—"

"And I'm only one," she said, wondering even as she said it why it seemed necessary to bait him.

Obviously Marc wondered too. He rubbed his forehead as if it had started to ache again. He explained slowly, enunciating clearly so that anyone over the age of three couldn't possibly misunderstand. "I'll just say this once. If I can't confront George and positively identify him so that an arrest can be made, a hell of a lot of people are going down the drain financially. Coming closer to home, I wouldn't plan on any old-age benefits from our firm, because I seriously doubt Keith and I will have any. Am I getting my point across now?"

"Loud and clear." Dana pushed her napkin on the table alongside her empty plate. "What do I have to do?"

"Just stay clear of me," Marc told her with unflattering directness. "With any luck, I can fade into the background, but you—" his glance swept over her, "you stand out in the crowd. Especially here on the island. Understand?"

"I don't need flash cards." She watched him sign the check, and pushed back her chair as he got to his feet. "Is it any use asking when you'll be back at the hotel?"

"Probably not until late. George doesn't usually start functioning until late in the day and since Michelle arrived in the middle of the night, they'll probably be sleeping in."

"All right." She walked beside him along the hotel corridor until they reached the turn-off to the elevator. "Aren't you going back to your room?"

He shook his head. "I have an appointment with the authorities in twenty minutes. We want to make sure all the paperwork is in order. George is bound to retain the best legal counsel available, so there can't be any loopholes." He glanced at his watch and then switched his attention to her face. "You will take care of yourself today, won't you?"

"I'm just one figure instead of eight," she quoted.

"Maybe, but some figures are irreplaceable as

far as I'm concerned. There isn't time to go into it now," he finished roughly. "I can recommend a tour of El Morro or the Pablo Casals Museum. I wish to hell I could go with you." Catching her by the wrist, he pulled her close and bent his head to kiss her hard. Releasing her almost immediately he said, "And if I learn that you've been chatting up any of the residents, I'll—"

"You'll what?" she asked with some difficulty because after that kiss her heart was pounding like a jackhammer.

"Damned if I know," he acknowledged with a grin, "but I'll think of something."

"And tonight," she asked when he started to walk away. "Your place or mine?"

"Definitely yours. I'll bring the champagne."

With that, he disappeared around the corner and Dana was left to try and get her breathing back to normal before attempting the stairs up to her room.

Chapter Eight

It was all very well to keep a stiff upper lip while bidding him farewell, she thought later as she wandered around the empty confines of her room, but it was hard trying to keep her spirits up. Marc hadn't mentioned the danger element again, but after what had happened to him the night before, she couldn't get it out of her mind.

She wandered around the room, grimacing at the still-dripping air conditioner and then looking out through the French doors onto the balcony. Another half hour and she'd be beating her head against the faded walls of the room. That only left going out and trying the tourist trail as Marc had suggested.

She knew it would be hot and humid during the day, but she still hesitated over leaving the room with just a pair of dark glasses to conceal her identity. While San Juan was a huge city, it was quite possible that Michelle Gonzalez might be shopping in the old city square for last-minute items that she'd had to leave behind.

Dana pursed her lips thoughtfully and then dug down into her suitcase to emerge with a wide-brimmed foldable straw hat that she generally used for sunning on the side of a swimming pool. She pulled it on and tucked her hair up out of sight. After putting her sunglasses on again, she gave a satisfied nod. The brim made it impossible for much of a view of her face, and Michelle would have to be at very close range indeed to identify her.

Dana took the stairs again going down to the lobby and avoided leaving her key at the desk, keeping it in her purse instead. The less the hotel knew about her comings and goings the better.

Once out of the hotel, she asked an artist sitting on a low stone wall nearby for directions to the center of Old Town and then strolled down the narrow cobblestone street.

At any other time, she would have been fascinated by the shop windows on either side. The wonderful jewelry displays and the names over a few of the doorways sent her eyebrows up. Evidently the Europeans had recognized a profitable outlet for their goods as well as the North Americans.

She lingered longest in front of a store with remarkable glass figures and then shook her head. That was all she needed—a heavy glass eagle or sailboat to carry home on the airplane. Marc would probably be tempted to hit her over the head with it. Her amused grin faded as she suddenly wondered if they would even *be* returning together or whether he'd be putting her on an earlier plane the way he did in Kentucky. The tight feeling came back to her stomach as her mind considered some of the unpleasant ramifications.

Probably it was the hot, sticky weather that was making her so despondent, she told herself. It was no wonder, when she could feel the perspiration soaking the back of her neck and dripping between her shoulder blades.

By then, she had turned into the main square of Old Town and paused to see if there were some place close where she could find a cold drink. There was a tiny grocery halfway down the square, but she didn't really want to linger on the curb while she enjoyed some refreshment.

She walked down the sidewalk, wondering if there would be an appetizing place on a side street, and then started to laugh as she noted some familiar arches a block away. Without wasting any more time, she headed for it. The purists might say that she was acting like the typical American tourist, but on the other hand, she knew exactly what she wanted to order.

The menu inside the establishment was printed in Spanish, but there wasn't any difficulty in getting some frozen yogurt and a refreshing glass of water. Since the air conditioning was working well, Dana was tempted to order a three-course meal and spend the early afternoon there. She removed her sunglasses before starting to eat and debated taking off her hat since it didn't seem probable that Michelle would be a potential cus-

tomer in that part of town. Still, there wasn't
any use taking chances, so she simply sat back
at a corner table and relaxed.

She consumed her yogurt as slowly as possible
and then left to walk back to the square where
there had been a cab rank. Fortunately, she
found a waiting taxi with a driver who understood the bare rudiments of English and promised a drive around the governor's mansion of La
Fortaleza with a look at San Juan Gate, even taking in the San Juan Cathedral, which apparently
contained the body of Ponce de Leon. Afterward,
they would cruise by El Morro.

When they got down to the important business
of setting a fare, Dana tried to dispel the driver's
idea that all visitors from the States were mil-
lionaires. A compromise was finally reached, and
concluded with the driver swinging open the
back door of his cab to gesture her inside. His
broad grin made Dana suspect that she'd come
off the loser in the financial discussion, but she
was too hot to argue any longer.

There was the semblance of air conditioning
in the cab and, since it was a leisurely tour, she
was able to ignore the Gran Prix maneuvers of
some San Juan drivers on the main thoroughfares.

Her driver faithfully followed all his promises
and, some hours later, inquired in broken English if she'd like to stop her sightseeing and
have some refreshment. It seemed his sister had
a small eating place.

Dana decided that anything would help the
time pass and indicated she was willing. When

he parked a few minutes later in front of a dingy restaurant not far from the fortress, she wondered if she'd made the right decision. Inside, however, the conditions were better, with red-checked tablecloths and a lively clientele. There was music blaring from a speaker over her head which fortunately prevented much conversation. After ordering a soda and a steak sandwich, Dana was allowed to sit and ostensibly enjoy the music while her driver sought out his sister and apparently caught up on the family gatherings.

That stop allowed another hour to pass and Dana decided that she did feel better after consuming some food. By then, she and her chauffeur were on excellent terms and she instructed him to let her off at her hotel rather than the city square.

It was as he was pulling up by the entrance that she noted a familiar feminine figure walking down the stone steps of the building, raising her hand to hail the very cab in which Dana was seated.

"Quick! Drive on!" Dana instructed her driver, bending over on the seat as she spoke.

"But *señora*," he objected, still braking. "This is your hotel."

"I don't want the hotel. Drive on! *Now!*"

Even if he didn't understand her reasoning, he couldn't miss the urgency in her voice and he obediently speeded up, leaving Michelle Gonzalez a few feet away from the curb.

Dana didn't sit upright again until they were halfway down the block and another car had pulled out of a parking space behind them. "Now—listen carefully," she instructed the driver. "I want you to go around the block. The woman who wanted this cab—you remember?"

As she paused, she met his eyes in his rear-view mirror and he gave her an annoyed look. "Naturally, *señora*. I could use another fare after I leave you."

"I promise more money. *Mas dinero*," she emphasized. "Just do as I ask. I want you to follow that woman if she gets another cab. *Comprende?*"

"*Si, si.*" The mention of money brought instant cooperation, and he cut sharply in front of another car on the narrow street to turn and retrace their route. "You don't want her to know? *Verdad?*"

"That's it," Dana said absently, looking anxiously out the window as they approached the hotel again from another side. Then, seeing the driver's perplexed expression, she said apologetically. "Sorry. You're absolutely right."

"Like the television—follow that car?" he asked, making sure.

"Right. Don't get too close to the steps," she warned. "Oh, good! She's still at the curb trying to hail a cab." Then, as she noticed the uniformed hotel doorman appear around the corner of the old building gesturing behind him, she said, "I take it back. She has help."

"There is a taxi rank up the block," Dana's driver said in a bored tone. "All she had to do was walk up the hill and find it."

"It doesn't matter now," Dana told him. "At

least we haven't lost her. When they drive off, don't get too close."

"*Señora,* even in Puerto Rico we see the same movies," he retorted as he let in his clutch and started off with a jerk.

Dana subsided nervously on the seat as he obediently pulled in the line of traffic two cars behind Michelle's cab. It was almost gridlock in the narrow street before they turned off to join a busy arterial headed back toward the airport. Dana mopped her forehead, thinking that either the car's air conditioning had stopped working or her nervous system was working overtime.

Marc's instructions at breakfast thudded in her ears and her conscience had trouble defending her actions. As much as Dana rebelled at his strict orders, she had to admit that she didn't know what she was going to do once Michelle got out of her cab.

Fortunately, Michelle seemed to like the crowded city environs because the cab ahead turned left again and was driving straight toward the elegant beach section of the island.

Modern hotels soon lined the road interspersed with expensive-looking restaurants and shops whose windows displayed designer outfits for play and sophisticated resort life. By then, the sidewalks were thronged for the cocktail hour and Dana gave silent thanks for Michelle's choice of destination.

They drove another block or two before Dana's driver slowed and then pulled over to the curb. "They've turned in over there," he said gestur-

ing toward the circular drive of a tall modern
hotel to their left. "Should I follow?"

"Let's wait here for a minute until I see if she's
getting out. Darn that fountain! I can't tell . . ."

"She's getting out, I think," the driver said,
leaning forward to peer through his window.
"Now she's going in the building and the cab is
leaving. What do we do now?"

Maybe it would be best to pay off her cab and
try to think what was next on the agenda as she
lingered by the cold drink stand on the sidewalk.
"You've been fine," Dana told her driver. "I can
handle things from here," she added, lying in
her teeth. "How much do I owe you?"

He hesitated, and then named a very fair sum.
Dana was careful to add a substantial tip as she
got out of the cab and thanked him.

Before he drove off, he leaned across the front
seat to say, "If you need to go back to Old Town,
that man," he gestured toward the smartly uniformed hotel doorman, "he can help you."

Dana smiled her thanks and watched him
drive off, cutting into the thick lane of traffic
with casual aplomb. Then she gave her brimmed
hat a tug so that it hid as much of her face as
possible and walked over to purchase a soda
from the soft-drink stand.

As she stood and sipped from a straw, she surveyed the hotel across the way more carefully.
There seemed to be a steady stream of people
going in and out of the entrance so that she
wouldn't stand out if she wandered in with her
head down.

She couldn't take the chance of a nosy reservations clerk by asking if there were a Michelle Gonzalez registered. On the other hand, there was wonderful anonymity in a call from a public phone in the lobby inquiring for the woman. And if Michelle answered, all she had to do was hang up.

The next best thing would be to call Marc's room at their hotel and see if he'd returned. Not for the first time, she damned the fact that he hadn't left a number where he could be reached during the day.

She put the empty soda bottle in a rack and then waited on the curb for a break in the traffic. A minute or so later, she decided that she'd be old and gray before anyone would acknowledge that a pedestrian had some rights. Fortunately, at that moment a teenager near her stepped off the curb, holding up his hand with an authoritative gesture. Dana scurried in his wake and drivers gave way in both directions, evidently deciding they didn't want two bodies in the street.

Dana made her way up the curving drive of the hotel trying to look casual. It seemed as if the doorman gave her a frowning appraisal when she went in the big glass doors, but she didn't linger to find out for sure.

Once in the huge lobby, she paused long enough to note the reservation desk was to the right, the patio and gardens exit was straight ahead, and to the left, two steps led up to what appeared to be a good-sized casino. That part of the hotel was obviously the drawing card at that time of day, with a steady stream of patrons headed toward the entrance.

Dana looked around for the public telephones and found a bank of them behind an imposing marble column en route to the ladies' restroom. It took a minute or two for Dana to discover a courtesy notepad which listed the name and telephone number of the hotel as well. She struck out when she was connected with the hotel operator, who spoke English haltingly. The name Gonzalez brought a complete blank as far as the hotel roster was concerned. At that point there was little Dana could do other than say "thank you" and hang up.

She told herself not to get discouraged. Considering the seriousness of the charges that Marc had mentioned, she really couldn't expect the couple to put their name up in neon lights at the hotel even if they were staying there.

Dana decided her options were still the same; if Michelle were still in the hotel she was bound to reappear in the lobby sometime.

Dana walked back into the lobby, trying to act nonchalant as she lingered over a display from the hotel's gift shop. Her glance went again to the casino entrance. From the looks of things it was possible to perch in front of a slot machine like any dedicated gambler and have an unobstructed view of the elevators and the lobby.

She checked the currency in her purse and decided that she could manage to stall for a while if she didn't lose too drastically and took her time pulling the handle on the one-armed bandit. Perhaps soon Marc would report back to his hotel room and she'd be able to ask what to do.

It didn't do to linger too long thinking about his answer to that, as she suspected it would be pithy and profane—probably ending in a concise order to run, not walk, to the nearest taxicab and not bother to pass "Go" on the way.

There was a scantily clad change girl inside the casino entrance. After a quick glance at a slot machine at the end of the row, Dana handed over some bills and requested the equivalent in nickels.

She sat down and tried to appear intent upon winning a fortune. After one pull of the handle, she scooted the stool around so that she could keep her glance on the lobby and elevators.

After that, the time passed slowly. Fortune smiled on her by paying back a few nickels in the course of things so that she could continue to play without suffering any drastic losses. The best part was that no one was paying the slightest attention to her.

As the minutes and finally hours went by, Dana's stomach sent notice that it would welcome any food that might come its way. She noticed that drinks were being served to the casino patrons on request and wondered if she could manage a sandwich on special order.

When a waiter ventured close, she put in a request. Food, he explained, would be available in the dining room which was on the other side of the lobby or out on the patio.

"I can't leave here," Dana countered, and gestured toward the stack of nickels in front of her. "I promised to meet my husband and he'll be terribly annoyed if he has to come looking for me." She rummaged in her purse and brought out a folded ten dollar bill which she deposited on the tray he was carrying. "Just a small cheese sandwich would be wonderful. Could you manage that?"

Her coaxing smile had persuaded men to change their minds before, and the waiter was no exception. The bill was palmed efficiently and he nodded. "I'll be back soon."

"Great. I'll be here," she assured him. And then as she watched him disappear down to the lobby she muttered under her breath, "Unless some of the Gonzalez family appear, and then I'm on my way."

At that point when she absently stuck another nickel in the machine, she was rewarded with a stream of nickels which had her neighbors looking enviously her way. Dana's eyes widened with delight as she scooped the overflow into her bag since there wasn't room on the tiny wooden shelf in front of the machine.

It was only five minutes later before her waiter reappeared, carrying her sandwich neatly disguised under a cloth napkin. He put it down on an empty stool nearby. "Would you like something to drink, *señora*?" he asked when it was arranged to his satisfaction.

Dana decided she'd be pressing her luck to try

for a cup of coffee so she shook her head. "No, thank you. The sandwich will be just fine."

He nodded and disappeared into the crowd of patrons who were playing the more expensive machines in the middle of the room.

Dana ate her sandwich one-handed, intent upon keeping up her role as the dedicated gambler. She'd just finished the last bite of crust and was using the camouflage napkin to wipe her fingers when a casual glance at the lobby showed both George and Michelle Gonzalez emerging from the elevator.

George looked nervous and his glance was searching the lobby. Dana dropped her head and stared straight at the machine in front of her, casually pulling the handle before allowing another sideways glance at the lobby.

By then, the Gonzalez couple had joined the crowd of people filing into the night club, which apparently was sandwiched between the casino and the patio. She'd noticed a big placard advertising the floor show in her earlier tour of the lobby, but it had never occurred to her that George and Michelle would spend any time at the early performance.

Dana chewed uncertainly on her lower lip as she watched them file through the doors out of sight. "Damn," she muttered, and then quickly collected the rest of her nickels by shoving them into her purse in a wholesale sweeping movement.

What she didn't anticipate was the fact that the purse weighed a ton when she attempted to slip the strap over her shoulder. The combination of her usual gear plus her winnings made the bag bulge like carry-on luggage.

For an instant she hesitated, wondering if she should seek out the cashier and change her loot into more manageable currency, and then the thinning lines of patrons going into the night club alerted her that she didn't have any time to waste.

She scurried back to the public telephones, resting her bulbous purse against her hip before dialing the number of her hotel so the operator could ring Marc's room. By the fifth unanswered peal she knew that her luck was out, but instead of hanging up when the hotel operator came back on the line, she said that she wanted to leave a message. "Would you tell him that I'm at the Hotel Belem," she said, "and that I'll meet him here."

"'Who shall I tell him called?" the operator wanted to know.

Dana thought furiously, reluctant to leave any clue as to her presence if someone was keeping a close watch on Marc. "Just sign it 'Dan-Dan,'" she said finally in desperation.

"*Como?*"

"Dan-Dan," Dana replied, enunciating carefully, and then hung up. She stood leaning against the telephone in the quiet alcove and tried to think. The chances were against Marc's ever getting the message, which meant she was on her own. And exactly what in the dickens was she supposed to do to apprehend a million dollar swindler and his wife? If things got too out-of-hand without Marc showing up, she possibly might have to resort to desperate measures. Hopefully in the next half hour, she might think of a few. She hitched her heavy purse onto her hip and started toward the night club entrance.

"You wish something, madame?"

Dana came back to reality as she realized that the dinner-jacketed doorman at the nightclub door wasn't going to let her by.

"I beg your pardon." Her annoyed response would have been more effective if she'd been dressed for the evening like the other patrons, who had dripped sequins and featured décolleté necklines. The doorman was giving her bulbous shoulder purse an especially derisive look.

"My friends have already gone in, honey," Dana said with a quick switch of tactics and accents. "I'm sure they left my name with you," she continued in the broadest Texan she could summon. "Or maybe it was your friend ovah-theah." She waggled a finger toward another man in a dinner jacket who was checking the pages of a ledger.

The man gave a look at the couples who had lined up impatiently behind Dana and then waved her through the door. "Go on in, madame. We're running late as it is."

Dana flashed him a meaningless smile and scurried through the foyer. As she opened another door into the interior of the club, she let out a gasp because it was like going from day into night.

Evidently the proprietors were trying for an

intimate atmosphere because the only illumination came from squat hurricane-type candles on the white tablecloths. A fire marshal would have a fit, Dana thought as she moved to the side of the doorway until her eyes became accustomed to the dimness. Not only was the illumination almost nonexistent, the hotel had shoved tables so close together that the patrons of one table practically had to inhale when their neighbors behind them were breathing out.

A moment or two later, Dana discovered another hazard; apparently the night club lovers in Puerto Rico were chain-smokers because blue smoke was hanging like Los Angeles smog in the candlelight.

"Good Lord," she muttered in disgust. For that dubious privilege, people were paying an arm and a leg in admittance fees. Overworked waitresses were trying to service the tables, announcing that two drinks would be served, simultaneously—Las Vegas style. That way, they could watch the ice melt in one while they tried to swallow the other, Dana recalled.

"'You are having trouble finding your friends, *señora*?"

It was the ledger-bearing man from the front entrance who'd pulled up beside her and was bestowing a very suspicious look.

"No." Dana managed a confident smile. "It was so dark that I've just located them. Over there on the far side of the room. Beyond the corner of the stage." She waggled her fingers at him provocatively before setting off purposefully around the back of the room.

Once past the first few tables, she glanced over her shoulder and was relieved to see that the man had apparently gone back to the foyer.

At that moment, a blast of music that could have been heard as far as Old San Juan sounded from the small stage. A red, well-worn velvet curtain parted to reveal a spectacular blonde who launched into a soprano version of "There's No Business Like Show Business." It only took Dana another minute to realize that the whole thing was lip-synced, trying to make up in volume for sparsity of talent. The good thing about it was that nearly every eye in the room was fastened on the blonde and the spotlight spilled off additional illumination so that threading through the tables wasn't quite so hazardous.

As the blonde launched into what surely must be the final chorus in a way that would have had Irving Berlin holding his head in shame, Dana realized she'd have to find a place to sit. Even the waitresses were giving her curious looks and it wouldn't take much for the maître d' to come inspecting.

There was an empty chair on the side of a nearby table for six and she sidled over to it. A second glance showed that the rest of the table was occupied by men who looked as if they lived in the neighborhood.

"Excuse me," she said brightly, hoping she sounded more confident than she felt as five pairs of eyes fastened on her when she hesitated by the empty table. "Is this chair taken?"

Five masculine voices responded in rapid Spanish and Dana's confidence sank still further. It didn't revive until the nearest man, who was middle-aged and fifty pounds overweight, rose to his feet and gallantly ushered her into the vacant space.

Dana beamed and sat down hurriedly as she saw the maître d' start to cruise the back of the room. "How nice of you-all," she said, giving her tablemates an expansive smile to show any onlookers she was finally among old friends. And it really didn't matter if there were a language barrier, she discovered a minute later, when the blonde segued into an arrangement of "Anything Goes" that made conversation impossible.

The man next to her happily pushed an extra drink toward her and Dana beamed back when she saw there was a line of untouched ones in the middle of the table. Finally, she thought in relief, she was one of the crowd. Now, all she had to do in the moments of flickering light, was to find where in the hell Michelle and George were located.

She took a sip of her drink and let her gaze wander around the room, trying to appear as if she were just casually interested in what was going on. It took the sudden awareness of a muscular arm around her shoulders to bring her back to the heavy-set man sitting beside her. No doubt about it—he belonged to the arm. Not only that, his gold-toothed smile showed that he believed everything was going according to schedule.

Dana wasn't quite sure what to do. Her overwhelming inclination was to give him a verbal dressing-down plus a sharp elbow in the ribs, but practicality made her hesitate. She needed her lookout spot and if she got too unpleasant, he would undoubtedly retaliate and send her on her way.

Compromise appeared to be the name of the game, she decided reluctantly as she felt the perspiration from his embrace gather on her shoulders.

She summoned a smile as she leaned forward in her chair and mimed a fanning motion with her hand. "*Caliente,*" she managed, and then wondered whether it should have been "*caldo.*" Her seatmate frowned for an instant as he lost contact, and then shrugged in agreement. Reaching for a cigarette from the package on the table in front of him, he politely offered one to Dana and then, after her refusal, lit up himself. She managed to keep a pleasant expression on her face although the feeble air-conditioning unit drew the smoke back to her. Looking for an upbeat thought, she realized that a cigarette would keep at least one of the man's hands occupied and above the table. Since she couldn't hope for that forever, she leaned forward with her elbows on the table and focused her attention on the stage.

By the end of the first set of nostalgic show tunes, Dana decided she not only had to worry

about her virtue but her hearing, as well. The
show manager had evidently decided that audience enthusiasm would be molded by high volume and he had it up to a point where a heavy
metal band couldn't compete. She managed to put
a finger in one ear under the guise of resting her
palm on her cheek, which made things temporar-
ily bearable. As she glanced around the audience,
she saw that most of them were screaming at
each other in sporadic conversations and consuming their drinks as quickly as possible.

As her neighbor's free hand disappeared below
the table, she thought, dear God, let me get out
of here before I stand up and start screaming.
Not that it would do her much good, she decided
as she tried to turn her back to him—nobody could
hear a banshee over that rendition of "Seventy-six
Trombones."

It was on the finale that an extra spotlight lit
up the ringside tables and she got a clear view
of Michelle and George. They were seated with
two men and weren't paying any more attention
to the singer and four newly added dancers than
she was. There was an attaché case on the table
in front of George and he was busily tucking
something away in it as the spotlight dimmed.

"Damn!" Dana murmured, forgetting that she
was pretending to be entranced by the floor
show.

"*Como?*" It was her seatmate of the heavy arm
and wandering fingers.

Dana decided that she'd have to try and reach
Marc again before there was any more "follow

that cab" stuff on her own. She started to stand up only to find that her neighbor didn't want to let his newfound friend desert him.

"No, no," he insisted, keeping the heavy arm on her shoulder and effectively pushing her back down in her seat. *"Por favor,"* he said earnestly, pushing another drink from the collection on the table toward her.

"No, thank you." It was hard to sound emphatic when the taped music started again. A quartet of dancers attired in abbreviated costumes with moulting maribou trim went into a high-kicking version of "New York, New York"—ostensibly to gratify any tourists in the audience.

When her seatmate's hand stayed in place, Dana made another try. Since she didn't know the word for ladies room and didn't know the charade for powdering her nose, she said, *"El telefono. Es necessario. Ahora."* She reared upward on the last word and found herself free at last.

Staying carefully out of his reach, she smiled at the group in general and beat as hasty a retreat as she could between the crowded tables. A quick look over her shoulder showed that her seatmate was sitting down again, apparently not willing to give up drinks and entertainment for an ungrateful *turista*.

The Gonzalez table was in darkness and Dana didn't see any point in hanging around to check that they were still in the audience. She'd make another phone call and then hover unobtrusively in the lobby or the casino.

It was so dark when the dance act ended that she lingered with her back to the rear wall of the room waiting for some illumination so that she could leave.

It was at that exact moment she felt a heavy hand clamp onto her forearm, freezing her in place.

Oh hell! Dana thought distractedly, her table partner had followed her after all. Well, the time for diplomatic chit-chat was over. "If you don't let go of me this very minute," she ordered in a tone that could be heard even over the music, "I'll stamp you into the ground and break you up in little pieces. Do you get that?"

"Loud and clear," snarled a familiar masculine voice in her ear. "But not until I have a chance at you. Just head for the door, lady. Don't attract any attention or I swear that there'll be a better floor show here than the one on the stage. Now— march!"

Chapter Nine

Dana was frogmarched out of the casino so quickly that her feet hardly touched the carpet. It wasn't until they were out in the deserted foyer where one of the night club captains was leaning against the wall and chewing on a toothpick that Marc loosened his grip.

Dana whirled to face him, all of the frustrations of the day coming to the fore. "Where in the hell have you been?" she snapped. "I've been trying all day to find you. At least since about five-thirty," she amended, seeing the ominous look he was sending her way.

"That's exactly why I didn't leave you my itinerary," he countered. "I had an idea you might do something idiotic. But never—" he held up his palm before she could interrupt, "never did I dream you'd be so damned foolish as to try and be in at the kill."

"You know that George and Michelle are in there?"

"Along with a couple of George's trusted buddies," Marc confirmed. "You didn't think that I was there for the floor show, did you?"

Dana noticed the nightclub captain's expression sharpen as he heard that and decided to change the subject quickly. "Hadn't we better get back in there? You might lose them."

Marc put out a hand to detain her when she turned back to the double doors. "You're not going near the place again. And I'm not handling this alone—unlike some people I could mention." His glance raked her again. "We're waiting till the end of the show before we close in so there won't be any rumpus."

"Well, then why can't I—"

"No way." He didn't let her finish the sentence, urging her down the steps to the lobby. "You, Miss McIntyre, are headed back to your hotel room and the dripping air conditioner."

Dana pulled to a defiant stop near the entrance to the casino and gestured toward that familiar territory. "At least let me wait up there." Her glance went to her nickel slot machine where a heavy-set woman was now pulling the handle. In front of the woman was a veritable mountain of nickels and even as she watched, another cascade came tumbling down. "Oh, damn!" Dana groaned.

"What's the matter now?"

"That was my machine. I nursed it along for hours and now she's getting the payoff. It isn't fair."

Marc shook his head as if he couldn't believe what he was hearing. "Obviously you got too much sun today. Come on, I can't waste any

more time. There's a taxi pulling up at the entrance right now."

Dana didn't have time for any more objections
as he trundled her past the big glass doors and
into the now-empty cab.

When the taxi started off, Dana looked through
her rear window and saw Marc disappear back
into the hotel. It simply wasn't fair, she thought.
He could at least have let her be in at the end
of things! Remembering the pile of nickels in
front of her slot machine, her lips tightened even
more. As things had turned out, she might as well
have skipped that dreadful night club show entirely. Especially since Marc clearly didn't appreciate her efforts in his behalf.

"You are not enjoying your stay in San Juan,
señora?"

The cab driver's anxious question cut into
Dana's consciousness finally and she met his
glance in the rearview mirror. "It's fine," she
said absently. "Just fine."

Seeing that she wasn't going to continue the
conversation, the driver shrugged and turned his
attention back to the traffic. So much for American women and their reputed free and easy
ways!

Dana simply leaned back on the cracked vinyl
seat and tried to relax. It wasn't easy after what
had happened. Marc hadn't even tried to listen
to her explanation, and she had expected at least
tepid appreciation for her efforts.

When she remembered, he had been pointedly unenthusiastic at her sudden appearance at

the hotel in San Juan. Her conscience surfaced
at that point, pointing out that it was probably
because he thought she'd be recognized and blow
the operation.

Dana flounced angrily on the seat, debating
whether that was his real reason for shoving her
in the background. Considering his business relationship with Keith, he might just be keeping
all his options open before taking her to the airport and sending her home.

Some fifteen minutes later, the car pulled up
in front of her hotel and Dana leaned forward to
check the fare on the meter. Smiling politely at
the driver, she opened her purse to search for
her wallet. The bag was still crammed with nickels from her slot machine and her wallet had to
be unearthed from beneath them. When she finally had it in her hand, she found only three
one dollar bills in it.

"I'm terribly sorry," she said to the driver as
she handed them over, "I'll have to give you the
rest in change."

A sudden frown creased his face. *"Como?"*

"Coins," she explained, running her fingers
through them and feeling like Fagin in the process. "I only have nickels."

He stared in disbelief as she started counting.
It took four heaping handfuls before she reached
the meter tab. The driver put up his palm in a
violent gesture when she started counting even
more for a tip.

"Nada mas," he ordered, and reached over the
back of his seat to open her car door. "G'night,

señora," he said forcefully and drove off with a
screech of tires, showing she would have still
been standing on the hotel curb at the beach if
he'd known what his payoff was going to be.

His reaction didn't do much for Dana's self-
esteem, which was already at an all-time low,
and she kept her eyes on the ground as she
mounted the worn stone steps of her hotel. It
took a familiar female voice to make her look up
suddenly and then dip her head again to hide
beneath the brim of her straw hat as she recognized Michelle Gonzalez getting out of a cab on
the far side of the steps.

A minute later, she saw that such caution
wasn't necessary because the brunette didn't
waste any time looking at the scenery before she
hurried up the steps and into the hotel foyer.

Dana glanced around cautiously to see if
George was also lurking near the shrubbery before hurrying up the steps behind Michelle.

She'd moved a little too fast because the
woman was just then retrieving a key from the
hotel clerk. Dana had to pull up and pretend a
sudden interest in a bulletin board of sightseeing
trip brochures near the door. Her straw hat disguise must have satisfied the other woman because Michelle just took a fleeting look in her
direction before heading for the elevator.

Dana lingered a moment longer in the foyer
and then turned toward the inside stairway.
Since there were only three flights to the hotel,
she'd go up to the top and work her way down,
checking out the corridors.

She took the stairs two at a time for the first flight and then in the more conventional way after the second floor landing. When she finally reached the third floor doorway, she was breathing like a wounded whale. All the way up the stairs, she'd been doing her best to decide whether or not she should intercept Michelle or just try another watching brief and hope that Marc would appear more quickly this time.

Opening the heavy fire door on the third floor landing, she abruptly found that the problem had been solved for her.

Michelle stepped into the stairway landing before Dana could move out into the corridor.

"My dear," the other woman purred. "That's what I like about you. You are so predictable. I knew when Marc showed up at the beach, that you'd probably be hanging around. Next time, don't try to hide under a silly hat brim. But I don't have any more time to waste on you—"

Michelle used the full force of her upper body to slam Dana's head into the heavy metal fire door behind her, moving so quickly that Dana was caught completely unprepared.

There was just a split second for Dana to realize what was happening before the back of her head collided with the door. Blackness fell over her like a shroud as she collapsed on the cement landing in a lifeless heap.

"For Pete's sake, woman, wake up."

The voice was familiar and masculine. The only thing new was a cascade of cold water spurting like a geyser into her ear and down her neck.

She focused with difficulty on Marc's hazy figure bending over her and muttered, "Oh God—my head! Stop trying to drown me."

Marc gave a snort of relieved laughter and sat up, still hanging on to a dripping face cloth. "I'm tempted, but I'd better wait until the doctor comes and gives me the go-ahead."

Dana pushed painfully up on an elbow, trying to figure out what she was doing in a strange room on a strange bed and with the grandfather of all headaches pounding under her damp hair. Then, abruptly, it all came back and she struggled to sit upright despite Marc's restraining arm. "That woman! I could kill her!"

"Simmer down." Marc soothed, pushing a couple of pillows behind her and forcing her back against the headboard. "I know how you feel. I came down the hall when you were colliding with that door. Believe me, Michelle is extremely sorry that she gave in to that impulse. There was a Puerto Rican detective with me and he didn't lose any time hauling her off to jail. A cell in San Juan is a far cry from the plush surroundings Michelle is used to."

"Great!" Dana said, attempting to stop the water which was still dripping into her ear. "And don't say anything to me about turning the other cheek."

"I wouldn't think of it," Marc said, getting up from the side of the bed to toss the damp face cloth into the bathroom basin. He came back to stand by the side of the mattress and stare down at her with a concerned expression. "How do you feel? Other than the obvious," he said hastily. "Any double vision or blackouts?"

"Not really. You don't have to worry, I won't sue you for extra hazardous duty."

A fleeting smile went over his face. "That's good. I'll even pay your doctor's bill."

Dana allowed herself to be diverted. "I don't need a doctor. I just need some aspirin and a chance to spend five minutes with that brunette of yours."

"She was never *my* brunette. Give me credit for more sense than that," he countered forcefully. "And right now, you couldn't punch your way out of the proverbial paper bag, so just lie there and relax."

"Or?"

"Or you might have a few bruises on your derriere to report to the doctor, as well."

"You wouldn't dare."

He didn't attempt to hide his amusement. "Want to try me?"

She settled back against the pillows, unwilling to continue a losing contest. "Tell me one thing before the doctor arrives—how did you manage to get here so fast? The last time I looked, you were headed back into the hotel on the beach."

"About two minutes after that, I saw Michelle going out a side door to the street. Apparently she didn't see any point in staying on a sinking ship with pal George."

"Just one more rat jumping overboard," Dana said with satisfaction.

A slow grin lightened Marc's expression. "Puss ... puss," he said reprovingly. "Obviously, yours wasn't a beautiful friendship even before she—"

"—tried to bash my head in." Dana put inquiring fingers to the area in question and winced. "You're right. She's a—"

A knock interrupted her, which was just as well, Dana decided. She watched with resignation as Marc moved over to the door and admitted a middle-aged man carrying a small black bag. "I'm Doctor Ramirez," he said to Marc, and then came over to Dana's bedside. "I understand you lost out to a door," he said, bending over her with a smile.

Dana, who had thoughts of trying to understand halting Spanish, smiled back thankfully. "You don't even have an accent," she told him.

"That's what comes from going to medical school in Pennsylvania. When I got back home, I found that I'm neither fish nor fowl." The twinkle in his eye showed that he wasn't taking any of it seriously. He used the same tone when he said casually over his shoulder, "Mr. Elliott, if you'll be kind enough to wait in the hall ..." The soft closing of the room door made him nod with satisfaction and bend over Dana again. "And now, Miss McIntyre, let's take a look at that poor head of yours."

The exam was thorough but rapid and he concluded by assuring her that she'd live to see another day. "I'l leave some pain pills with Mr. Elliott," he said, snapping his bag closed. "Don't try any Olympic marathons for the next day or so. Get as much rest as you can in the meantime."

Marc came back into the room a few minutes later, holding a small plastic vial of pills in front of him. "I'm to treat you very carefully and let you have two of these every four hours as needed." His voice sobered. "You look as if they might be needed now."

"You do wonders for a woman's ego," Dana said. "I'd look a little better if I could dry off and borrow your comb."

As she started to get up, Marc moved quickly to the side of her bed. "Are you sure this is a good idea?"

The ceiling light fixture seemed to sway alarmingly when Dana first attempted getting vertical, but it settled down again after she stood clutching Marc's arm. "It's okay," she told him breathlessly.

"Nevertheless, I'll leave the door ajar," he announced, steering her toward the bathroom.

"And if you hear me hitting the tiles—"

"I'll change our flight reservation and call the doctor back."

His remark about sharing the same airplane made Dana's headache subside momentarily. A look into the mirror over the basin brought it back again as she saw a reflection which seemed all pale cheeks and shadowed, haunted eyes. The wet hair on one side of her head didn't help either, and Dana decided that combing it back from her face was the best she could do.

"Are you still all right in there?"

Marc's worried tone made her eyes widen and then narrow thoughtfully. For an instant, it sounded as if he really cared.

"Dammit-all, Dana . . ."

She could hear his footsteps approaching and quickly pulled the door wide. "Sorry. I'm fine. I was just admiring the air conditioner. This must be your room."

"Because it doesn't leak?"

She started to nod and then decided that wasn't such a good idea. Marc saw her painful grimace and steered her gently but firmly onto the bed again.

"Hey, I'm not sleepy," she protested.

"I didn't say you had to close your eyes," he told her, reaching over to arrange the pillows behind her.

"That's good, because I still want to know what's been going on all this time. Michelle must have thought that I had the scoop or she wouldn't have turned on me."

Marc looked across at the worn chair by the French doors and finally settled at the end of her bed. "I hope you don't mind sharing," he said.

"Not a bit—except for your mosquitoes."

"They come later in the night." He surveyed her with narrowed eyes and apparently reached a favorable conclusion. "You must be feeling better."

"Practically back to my fighting weight." Dana was lying in her teeth, but things were going so well, it was worth the effort.

A slight smile appeared momentarily on his stern features, showing that he could read her thoughts very well, but he didn't contradict her. "Getting back to Michelle—"

"As so many men apparently have," she murmured.

"I wouldn't know about that. As far as I was concerned, she was simply George's live-in companion."

Dana's lips parted in amazement. "You mean they weren't married?"

"Not if a few of George's earlier comments are to be believed." Marc concentrated on pleating the fringe of the chenille bedspread. "I'm inclined to believe him. He's not one for sharing, and the thought of community property would send him fleeing in the opposite direction."

"So Michelle simply went along for the ride and what other goodies she could collect. From what I saw of her wardrobe, she got her share."

"George could well afford it. If he hadn't gotten greedy, he'd still be in clover."

"Which takes us back to Kentucky," Dana said pointedly.

"I hadn't forgotten. You're sure you want to hear the rest of this now?"

"Absolutely. And then I want to forget about the Gonzalez family."

"Fair enough. I didn't mention all of the background at breakfast. You've probably heard that the Kentucky racing stables have had a hard time of it in the last six months or so. The price on their yearlings has dropped drastically and some of the biggest syndicates have gone into chapter eleven. George wasn't directly affected, but he saw which way the wind was blowing and started some innovative bookkeeping in his company. That steered a good deal of the profits into his dummy accounts."

"I still don't see the connection—"

He held up his palm. "Take it easy. I'm getting to it. At first, George just planned to pick up some choice real estate at rock-bottom prices if the racing stables were forced to sell."

Dana frowned. "I can see where skimming accounts is fraudulent but—"

Her voice trailed off when Marc leaned forward and put a firm finger across her lips. "I told you to be patient. Just what George wasn't. He wanted things to move faster and figured out a way to compound his profits. He decided to move from the purchase of racing real estate to include a major industrial sector." Seeing Dana's puzzled expression, he moved his finger up to gently flick the end of her nose. "That was when he started some rumors about the industrial property being taken over as a nuclear dump site. He circulated those fake memos about the nuclear decision on official government letterheads to help his cause along. Uncle Sam frowns on that—it comes in the same category as counterfeiting fifty dollar bills or printing postage stamps—and the authorities came calling. George realized he'd gone too far then and decided to leave the country in a hurry."

"But why did he stop off here?"

"To collect the money from his extracurricular bank accounts. He wanted plenty to take with him to South America."

"And you got in the way," Dana said soberly.

Marc nodded. "All I was supposed to do was stall him in Kentucky—give the authorities a little more time to get their proof together. That's one reason I thought the wife and child idea might be good camouflage."

"And besides, you needed a sitter for John."

"Not really." Marc was sitting so close beside her on the edge of the mattress that Dana could feel his arm resting next to her thigh. "John simply helped my cause along. Incidentally, my brother-in-law's getting along fine and will be out of the hospital in the next day or so."

"Thank heaven for that," Dana said fervently, before her brow wrinkled again. "I don't understand though—"

"It's simple enough," Marc cut in impatiently. "I had planned to recruit you all along. The baby-sitting bit was just icing for the cake."

A warm sensation suddenly centered in Dana's midsection and she didn't have time to concentrate on her headache. "But why?"

"Because I needed an excuse to see you again. After that one disastrous date we had, I knew there was lots of ground to make up. Under ordinary circumstances, you probably wouldn't have come within thirty feet of me. If I could convince you that I needed your help—"

"—you were prepared to lie in your teeth to suit the occasion," she finished for him.

"Right. But then I suddenly found myself with John and I really did need some help." As her eyebrows rose, he gave a reluctant crooked grin. "Well, some specialized help. And everything went along fine until I invaded John's bath one morning and saw you in that wet, clinging robe. After that, I had a hell of a time keeping my hands off of you."

Dana was feeling the same way just then, but was determined not to let him off too easy. "Something you'd overlooked in your preplanning, no doubt."

"You could say that. Thank God, you're feeling better. When I saw Michelle shove you into that door, I'll never forget how I felt." His hand moved absently to caress her thigh. "I had an old-fashioned courtship in mind and instead I almost got you killed."

"You weren't to blame for that," Dana replied, trying to stay very still so that he wouldn't take his hand away. "If I hadn't decided to follow you to Puerto Rico, there wouldn't have been any problem."

"You have a point there." He gave her a thoughtful look. "Why did you come?" As she hesitated, he went on urgently, "The truth, Dana—I'm tired of fencing."

She managed a crooked smile. "That makes two of us. All right, Mr. Elliott—I decided that

I liked your courtship so much that I didn't want to let you out of my sight. Although I was scared to death that you'd simply shut the door in my face last night."

"Instead, you had to take care of me." He gave a grimace of annoyance. "Believe me, when I dreamed about sharing a bed with you the first time, I didn't plan on needing a night nurse."

"And now the situation's reversed." Her lips twitched with rueful laughter. "I might have a relapse so I don't think I'm well enough to be left alone tonight."

"I don't plan on leaving you alone for the next fifty years or so, my dear and dearest Miss McIntyre." He leaned over and gave her a soft kiss before sitting upright again. "If it's all right with you, I'd like to put a new gold band on your finger tomorrow in Las Vegas. That way, I might be able to break my habit of taking two cold showers a day."

Dana's heart was pounding so fast that it was difficult for her to answer. Especially when her imagination changed those separate cold showers into a lovely shared warm one.

"Darling?" Mac's voice had an undercurrent of worry. "I'm not rushing you too much, am I?"

"Oh, no!" Her response was so fast and fervent then that his tense expression abruptly relaxed. It returned an instant later when she went on solemnly, "Provided you agree to a couple of really important conditions."

Something about her voice must have given

her away because his eyes crinkled with laughter as he said, "Just name them."

She held up a slender finger. "One—sometime in the next year or so, you promise to try and provide John with a new cousin that looks just like him."

"I've already put it on the top of my list," Marc agreed, "and possibly another Dan-Dan later on." His caressing hand moved upward. "What's the second provision?"

"That you'll see if there's an earlier flight to Nevada." She clasped his hand against her breast, postponing the joy ahead. "Otherwise, the way I feel now, my love, we might not make it to the church for a week or so."

Marc found there was a nonstop to Las Vegas which left San Juan two hours later.

They were early for the plane.

27 million Americans can't read a bedtime story to a child.

It's because 27 million adults in this country simply can't read.

Functional illiteracy has reached one out of five Americans. It robs them of even the simplest of human pleasures, like reading a fairy tale to a child.

You can change all this by joining the fight against illiteracy.

Call the Coalition for Literacy at toll-free **1-800-228-8813** and volunteer.

Volunteer Against Illiteracy. The only degree you need is a degree of caring.